❦

A Slip in Time

An Historic Adventure
at the Benton Harbor Ship Canal

Other books by
Kathryn S. Zerler

Talk of the Towns, 1991

On the Banks of the Ole St. Joe, 1990

Love Poems for Dreamers, 1981

Blended Pleasures, 1981

It Must Be Angels, 1973

A Slip in Time

*An Historic Adventure
at the Benton Harbor Ship Canal*

By Kathryn Schultz Zerler

Historical Consultant *Nancy Watts-Stiles*
Cover design by *Vicky Nemethy*
Book design by *Joann Phillips*

Acknowledgements

For their encouragement and support, I wish to thank

Cynthia Cooke
David Stuebe
Marilyn Unruh

For Glenn Zerler

Love is the greatest gift.

Four corners, four seasons
Two persons, two reasons.
One space in the past
A place that will last,
Forever.

A Slip in Time

Contents

Part One: From the Present

Part Two: To the Past

Part Three: And Back Again

PART ONE:
FROM THE PRESENT

FROM THE PRESENT

My soul reached out to help her
So kind, so fine, so sure
Like golddust from a rainbow
Lovetrust from long ago.

I touched her life just barely.
I almost was not there
Like angel wings and gentle things
Of poems, songs and heartstrings.

Cynthia Marigold

❦ *Chapter One*

CYNTHIA MARIGOLD

Maggie was ringing up the sale of three books for a woman at the counter. Two more customers stood behind her in line. Maggie's eyes widened almost imperceptibly in relief as Karla took a place on the other side of the cash register, but her smile never faltered as she chatted with the customer.

Karla nodded a greeting to her store manager and pulled out a sheet of Christmas paper that said "Ho! Ho! Ho!" in bright green letters. She began wrapping the package of books as Maggie handed them over to her.

Doily strolled over purring like a finely tuned Mercedes. The black and white cat wound herself around Karla's ankles in a happy greeting, then sauntered elegantly away from the busy cash register to one of her favorite cat nap spots nearby. When Karla was in the store, Doily kept her in sight.

Maggie rang up the next sale and handed it over to Karla for wrapping. With one cash register, the buddy system seemed to work best.

Karla and Maggie helped the next two people in line, and six more — all with arm loads of books — who stood in front of the counter.

The Christmas week rush, Karla thought; sales from this season would pay her bills for the next two months. The bell attached to the front door jangled open and closed, the telephone rang and traditional Christmas carols from Karla's cassette player pervaded the store. Through all of the cacophony, Doily slept; only her ears moved toward certain sounds like tiny sonar satellite dishes.

They made change, wrapped packages, smiled and chatted with their customers. There was little time to assist people in selecting gifts and there was no need, people would buy anything at this time of the year.

They stayed open until eight o'clock that evening. "I'll open up tomorrow," Karla said. "You sleep in."

"I won't be too late; this morning they were waiting outside the door when I arrived," Maggie replied. She had worked in the store since before Karla purchased it when Mrs. Ritenberg retired. Karla could not remember working there without Maggie. Both women loved the curious women's bookstore and its eccentric regular customers.

"Be prepared for another busy morning. Only one shopping day left." Maggie said, waving good-by.

"I will; thanks Maggie."

Karla filled Doily's food and water bowls, locked up and walked to her apartment. The street lamps were wound with red ribbon, natural garlands and tiny white twinkle lights. Karla could smell the scent of pine as she moved past the poles. There were still a few shoppers hustling toward their cars, hauling neatly wrapped gifts that would be ripped open in two days.

A pile of Christmas cards lay on the floor beneath her letter slot. She picked them up and shuffled through the red, white and green envelopes glancing at the return addresses. It was nice to receive personal mail from people she knew instead of the usual bills and bulk mail. Karla put the cards on her bed to savor later when she had more time.

Now, she was looking forward to the pleasant rituals of Cynthia's winter solstice.

There were nine women in Cynthia's circle. Karla surveyed the cars as she approached Cynthia's house. Dodie was here; Barb probably rode with her. Roberta's new BMW was parked next to Dodie's four-year-old Chevrolet. At this hour it was likely that Karla would be the last to arrive. Good, Karla thought, most of the women were not here tonight; a small group would be easier to take after the hectic chaos of the Christmas whirl.

Cynthia lived about two miles outside of downtown St. Joseph, close enough for Karla to walk. The house was convenient to city services, yet private and somewhat remote, which was good for Cynthia since she had a tendency to sing loudly and play musical instruments late at night.

Located on an old brick road that ended just past her prop-

3

erty, the house was bordered on one side by two empty lots and surrounded in the back by a fragrant pine forest. Tonight, it looked like a Christmas card. Smoke curled from the chimney and drifted toward the moon. The cozy smell of burning wood wafted in the cold night air.

Karla knocked lightly on the door before stepping inside. She left her boots on the mat in the entry; the thick socks she was wearing would be warm enough in Cynthia's snug house. Dodie was the first to notice Karla's arrival.

"How's the weary retailer?" Dodie asked giving Karla a big hug. Dodie was an investment banker with a background in music. She was sharp in the financial world, yet sensitive to the person behind the checkbook. According to Cynthia, Dodie was nicely balanced.

"Definitely weary," Karla answered. "It's getting vicious out there."

"Tell me about it," Dodie said. "As far as I'm concerned, people are pulling far too much cash out of their accounts right now. Worse yet, they're running their credit cards to the upper limits. Not smart. The economy indicates more conservative spending."

"Lucky for me, most people don't heed the economy."

"Karla! Merry Christmas!" Barb exclaimed. She hugged Karla and led the way back into Cynthia's living room, where logs glowed in the wood stove and groups of oil lamps decorated the room with gentle tongues of light.

"Let me look at you," Karla said admiring Barb's attire. "The gloves are an excellent touch. You have definitely outdone yourself with this outfit."

"You like it?" Barb asked, twirling around. She made a mockery of modeling with the broad grin that spread across her face and stayed there, imposing and alone, like the grin of the Cheshire cat, until Barb took it back, replacing it with her own genuine smile.

Stephanie Barberas, "Barb" to her friends, was the chief costume designer for the Twin City Players. It was a job she loved and lived to the hilt; nothing was sacred to Barb, she had created costumes with everything from ruffles, lace and gloves to plastic spiders and lots of buttons. If it wasn't too big and didn't run away too fast, Barb had sewn it on clothing. She reveled in the concept of wearable art.

"It's a fabulous outfit; on you, it looks like a piece of kinetic sculpture," Karla answered. She felt close to Dodie and to Barb. Both women possessed a great deal of talent and intelligence, yet they each wore a mantle of vulnerability that made Karla want to reach out and reassure them that they were wonderful, cherished friends.

"Where are Roberta and Cynthia?" Karla asked.

"In the kitchen. Cynthia is preparing a special solstice supper for us. I brought a fruit salad and Barb made her famous spinach rolls," Dodie said, pouring a glass of wine from the carafe on the coffee table. She swirled the clear liquid around the insides of the generous goblet, releasing its bouquet just under her nose. Obviously pleased with the wine ritual, Dodie smiled at Karla and took a tiny sip.

"Chardonnay, dry the way you like it. May I pour?" she offered.

Karla accepted the wine — one glass, she promised herself — and settled into one of Cynthia's overstuffed chairs. Miss Kitty jumped to her side and perched on one of the chair's generous arms. Karla stroked the cat's furry neck and tried to identify the tantalizing smells coming from the kitchen. A fragrance of garlic wafted deliciously over the scent of baking bread.

Cynthia's house was a combination of comfortable antique furniture and colorful pieces made by local artists. The few walls in the open rooms were hung to the ceilings with paintings and tapestries. Cynthia had designed the structure and supervised the construction to her specifications. There was no plywood, glue or artificial material used anywhere in the house. It consisted entirely of natural wood, stone and glass. Cynthia had said she wanted the house to breathe on its own. The unvarnished wooden floors expanded and contracted with the seasons, big windows let in lots of light, and warmth from Cynthia's three wood-burning stoves provided the only source of heat.

Barb was talking about the new show she was working on. Karla drifted in and out of the conversation enjoying the hum of

5

friendship, the crackle of the logs and the mingled scents of cooking food. Miss Kitty's tail twitched contentedly as she purred and Karla felt the stresses of her family and the Christmas retail rush peeling away like days on a calendar. She stroked the nape of Miss Kitty's neck and sipped the wine; the well-aged taste of oak from the barrel soothed her, she savored its dry touch on her tongue.

When Cynthia and Roberta emerged from the kitchen, Karla was totally relaxed. Roberta looked like a striking Snow White in a red velvet tunic and leggings. With her white skin and black hair cut in a page-boy, Roberta personified the famous Disney character.

Cynthia spread her arms out wide in a gathering motion. Her body exuded strength and permanence, the smooth texture of her skin radiated from the warmth of the oven and the exertion of cooking.

"The food will keep until we are finished," Cynthia announced in a voice that both suggested and commanded authority. "Please come and be together around the circle."

A plush round rug of winter white wool lay in the center of Cynthia's dining room. She had arranged a small pile of clean straw at its hub. An altar to "the goodness and spirituality within all people" — one of Cynthia's firm beliefs and stock phrases — stood at the north quarter of the circle.

Karla placed a green candle upon the altar and three cloth bags of dried marigold seeds along the edge of the straw. She had dried the seeds in the fall with the intent of sharing them with friends. Even her minuscule window box garden always produced more than she needed. The other women also brought candles representing themselves to the altar and items symbolizing new life and sharing to the straw nest in the center of the room.

"This — our annual winter solstice — is the first passage into awareness," Cynthia said, looking at each woman in turn. She lit a stick of sage wrapped with string and cast the circle with a simple gesture, blowing smoke into the four corners of the room, the four directions of the universe. She moved gracefully, bending to light four white candles at the four quarters of the circle. There was no other light in the room, the candles illuminated the space with soft shadows that shifted slowly as the women moved.

"Tonight is the night of the longest dark, the turning point toward the return of new life. Endings are always beginnings. We approach hope and potential. A nurturing light glows warmly, brilliantly, within all of our hearts, outshining the darkness. Let your light touch our Mother Earth in all directions reaching out to those who live in the north, the south, the east and the west."

When Cynthia finished casting the circle she sat down on the straw in the center. Her muscular legs folded comfortably into a crosslegged position. The other four women sat down within the circle leaving a place for Cynthia at its edge.

"My hope for the future is for more laughter," Cynthia said from her perch in the middle. She smiled broadly; her blue eyes, bright in the candlelight, recognized each of the women in turn. Cynthia had the ability to make everyone, even in a crowded room, feel as if she was speaking only to them. She placed her palms on her folded knees and rocked slowly with a whimsical motion.

"I want to encourage laughter in others by laughing more myself, softly at first, laughing and smiling with my eyes, my ears, my nosehairs, everything! Urging others to laugh by accepting their special sense of humor and their special place on Earth. That's all." Then, Cynthia laughed. The deep chuckle coming from inside her belly was infectious — like all grins and giggles — and the other women laughed with Cynthia as she moved to her place on the circumference.

The room became still again and quiet as Karla entered the hub. She sat down on the straw amid the gifts of hope, which represented the sharing and new life to come, and listened for a moment to the rhythmic rise and fall of her own breath. Then she said, "My hope for the future is to create peace on Earth beginning with my sister, Doreen — a tall order, to be sure. My wish is for tolerance that I will accept her unconditionally and not fall into the old patterns of sarcasm that sting and linger."

Karla paused and thought for a moment. There were more words to be said about sarcasm, but she did not wish to preach.

7

She moved to the edge of the circle and sat curled up with her arms around her knees. As she hugged herself, she sent breath to each part of her body, appreciating and accepting her arms, elbows and hands, right down to her fingertips. She consciously directed her breath past her waist to her stomach, hips, thighs, knees and feet; where would I be without them, Karla thought? This is a good body, and every part works for the whole. She felt completely relaxed and at ease. The Christmas rush at Covers was gone from her mind; and so were her problems with Doreen. Karla felt fully in the present; she listened to Dodie, Barb and Roberta with full attention.

When each woman had taken her turn on the nest and returned to the circumference, a peaceful presence emanated from all of them, forming a powerful energy within the room. Karla thought she could almost touch it if she tried, but she did not wish to lift even a finger. No one moved. Not a sound save their deep, relaxed breathing could be heard.

In time, from her corner of the carpet, Cynthia began humming a familiar tune. The sweet sound was infectious and the others began to sing softly, rising from the circle one by one. Each woman lit her own candle, and as the light increased in the room, they joined hands. Karla felt an increased inner strength coursing through her outstretched arms as the women danced together around the circle. She saw the auras of Dodie, Barb, Roberta and Cynthia as pale white body halos. Their auras were glowing rings that draped each woman from head to foot and shielded them from harm.

Karla wished that the others could also view the dancing auras that were so prevalent to her. Every person had one, and it was unfortunate, thought Karla, that so few people were empowered to see them. Cynthia frequently said that Karla was in touch with another plane of vision and understanding. But Karla did not understand auras; she simply saw them.

Now, she felt the energy rising from the circle, generating toward an invisible cone above their heads. They raised their hands to reach for it, swaying like young trees in the winter wind.

When they had stretched and danced until each one felt filled with the power to carry out her wishes, they knelt with palms

8

open upon the floor to release the excess energy they had created and to ground themselves to the Earth once more. The circle was opened and each woman selected an item from the nest symbolizing the renewal of life. Karla picked up a drawstring bag and opened it. It contained a bar of lavender soap, Dodie's scent; she pressed the open bag to her face with both hands and breathed deeply of the delicate perfume. She would bathe with it later and enjoy its light, old-fashioned fragrance.

Cynthia gathered the items remaining from the ritual into a large cotton cloth. She placed sage ashes in the center, then candle wax and the straw. Drawing the four corners of the cloth together, she tied it with a string and placed the bundle near the front door.

Karla followed Cynthia to the kitchen and turned up the gas flame under a pot of wild rice and mushrooms which Cynthia had started earlier. Barb unwrapped her spinach rolls and put them into the oven to warm. Dodie scooped generous helpings of her fruit salad into bowls.

Roberta came into the kitchen and took a serrated knife from Cynthia's kitchen rack; she began to cut the whole wheat bread she had baked into thin slices, letting them drop like dominoes onto the wooden cutting board.

"You know," Roberta said thoughtfully, "I don't mean to generalize, but if my husband was here, he wouldn't have the vaguest notion of what to do. His intentions would be good, but he would stand around and not know what needs to be done. I think it's so great that we all understand how to pitch in and get the jobs done."

"I know what you mean," Dodie said. "There are so few times in life when a leader isn't necessary. To me, that's the ideal; people working together for a common cause, without bickering and with no one giving orders."

"Amen." Barb added. "Carrie sets the table every night, but I always have to remind her to do it. I wish that, someday, she would come home from school, do her homework, and then set the table without being asked."

"That's what friends are for," Karla said, "to give us a break from our families once in a while.

9

"And our jobs," Dodie said.

"And the public," Cynthia added.

They finished the preparations, talked, laughed, and enjoyed the delicious feast. They cleaned up the table together, making light work of the task. Again, there was no need for a leader, no one had to give orders, each woman knew what needed to be accomplished and she helped in her own way.

When it was time to depart, Cynthia motioned Karla to stay. Karla was bone tired. She looked at Cynthia questioningly.

"We need to talk. Something is about to happen and you are the only one who can help me . . . " Cynthia said. The words floated out of her mouth and drifted up like tiny stars. Her aura seemed to spark with their meaning. She was excited and intense, but in the same moment she recognized Karla's fatigue and amended her request. "You look like you need a good night's sleep, Cifelli. I'll come over in the morning."

"I have to open the store in the morning," Karla protested lamely. She could hear the weakness in her tone even as she attempted to dissuade her friend.

"I will come before then . . . at eight o'clock sharp . . ."

Karla nodded. It was pointless to argue with Cynthia once she had her mind made up. Besides, Karla was curious. Most encounters with Cynthia contained an element of adventure, and this occasion, like many others before it, seemed filled with promise.

❦ *Chapter Two*

ALL WE HAVE IS WITHIN US

When Karla returned from the YWCA the next morning, Cynthia was already in the apartment. She was slowly pouring boiled water into a filter of coffee. The aroma of freshly ground French roasted beans dripping into the hour-glass carafe greeted Karla as she walked into the kitchen.

"This must be a big favor," Karla said, fingering her wet, brown curls with both hands. "I can't remember the last time you were up and about this early. That coffee smells terrific."

"It's French vanilla. Did you swim?" Cynthia asked without looking up from the carafe. She was trying to pour in enough water to keep the coffee dripping steadily without floating the grounds. The shaggy layers of her blond hair fell around her face as she concentrated on filling the chemist's carafe with the correct amount of water.

"I had the pool all to myself," Karla replied, hanging a damp towel on a rack near the door. "Most people are too busy for physical fitness at this time of year, which is great for me; I relish the solitude of an empty pool. It's a luxury."

Cynthia poured two mugs of coffee and carried milk from the refrigerator to the table. She motioned Karla to a chair.

"Hm-m-m, you smell like lavender, it's a lovely scent . . ."

"It was Dodie's gift of renewal from last night," Karla replied accepting the mug. "I picked it from the selection in the nest. Thank you, again, by the way, for a refreshing evening. I needed it."

"Didn't we all. Karla . . ." Cynthia looked intensely into Karla's eyes as she spoke. She seemed to send out eyebeams that locked Karla's eyes onto her own. "You know I have a gift for

11

reading people. Sometimes I even feel slightly psychic. But not usually . . ." She let the sentence trail off, but she did not take her eyes off of Karla's.

Karla wondered what was going on — Cynthia's tone of voice was complicated, even for her. Karla's thoughts drifted to the possibilities, her practical mind listed them automatically: 1) Cynthia had a new boyfriend, 2) she was changing careers, giving up wellness counseling for something else, 3) she was moving to another city.

But, none of the options seemed to fit the intensity of Cynthia's mood or her insistence on seeing Karla immediately. This must be important. Cynthia was well aware of the last-minute Christmas rush in the retail business; she would not ask Karla for an idle favor at this time of the year.

"I have always felt that I am a receiver, you and I have talked about it," Cynthia said. "But for the most part, I truly could not swear that I had received most messages until after they arrived and I made some sort of a connection . . . does that make any sense? Well, no matter. This week I received two very definite visions that were so strong we cannot deny them." Cynthia paused and took a sip of the strong coffee she had carefully prepared.

Karla noticed the word *we* and shifted in her seat. She caught the pleasant scent of lavender in her movement.

Cynthia continued speaking. Her tone and posture were firm and deliberate. "The two visions were identical and they were not dreams, Karla, both of them came to me during the day when I was fully awake. Each time the message was urgent: there are two women who need our help. I could not see their faces and I do not know who they are, but we will know when we go back ."

"What do you mean, when *we* go back?"

"A slip in time. I know where one is. Actually they're all over and I've read about them and heard tales about them; but I've never received news of one myself. I've always longed to, of course. And now I have!" Cynthia could not keep the excitement out of her voice; Karla saw her aura pulsating like a shooting star around her. "The thing is, we have to go through it together. The visions were very explicit about that. Karla, you and I are going back to the year 1895."

"You and me?" Karla asked. She felt herself catching Cynthia's enthusiasm and it scared her; she wondered fearfully what she might be getting herself into. She knew from past experience that she was usually powerless to say no to Cynthia.

"Definitely. You figured prominently in the visions. Are you ready?" Cynthia's optimism was so tangible, it seemed to lift her to her feet. She stood up and headed toward the door. The muscles in her body fairly bristled with excitement. Karla could feel the goose bumps rising on her own skin.

"You mean now?" Karla asked. Her hand unconsciously moved to her head. She fingered her wet curls and stared at Cynthia. Karla watched as the blue of Cynthia's eyes widened to the outer limits of her eyelids.

"We have to go before noon today. It has to happen after the solstice ritual and before twelve noon on the next day."

"Cynthia, it is Christmas Eve. The store is nuts. I absolutely cannot go today, Maggie would kill me if I took off and left her in the lurch."

"She will never know you're gone. No one will. When we slip through time — no matter how long we spend in the past — only seconds elapse in the present. Our bodies will be here, but our spirits will travel through time, back to the year of 1895."

Karla stared silently at Cynthia. She trusted Cynthia's judgment and intuitions implicitly, but a slip through time? Going back to 1895? Right now?

Karla, too, had heard and read about the slips in time. She had always associated the descriptions of them with atmospheric passages for angels who needed to come and go to assist humans in need. The slips allowed those who traveled inside of them to carry perspective and knowledge to and from other time periods.

Karla knew that she herself had been assisted on several occasions by angels traveling through time; there had been so many incidents when she had said or done the right thing without knowing logically or emotionally what the correct response might have been. Now Cynthia was offering her a chance to become an angel herself for someone waiting in the year 1895.

13

"I was definitely a part of your vision?"

"No question. We must travel together and I know exactly how to do it . . ." Cynthia's wide blue eyes narrowed momentarily. "However, I have never actually completed the ritual . . ."

"What happens if . . ."

"The worst that could happen is we couldn't get through." Cynthia said intercepting Karla's question. "You know it's a protected ritual. I would be devastated if that happened. Not literally, of course."

Karla studied Cynthia's aura. It was pale yellow in color and not moving at all. Karla saw a soft glow around Cynthia's body. It was a calming aura and unusual for Cynthia, especially given the current circumstances. Karla compared what she saw now with the blazing quality of Cynthia's aura only moments before. It had mellowed from a shooting star to something akin to the first light of a sunrise, the prelight, pale and warm, before the sharply glinting rise of the full sun.

"What happens when we get there?" Karla said. She put her watch on, chugged the last of her coffee, and stood up to get her jacket.

"We become a part of women living in 1895. It is the phenomenon that makes some people so much wiser or more talented than others. When we enter into the women waiting for us in the past, they will immediately gain our knowledge. Then, when we depart, they will retain a part of us and we will carry a part of them back here with us.

"Karla, I know you," Cynthia continued with conviction. "You are an old soul. You've been on the receiving end of this already but receivers generally don't perceive it. Or they perceive it, but they do not grasp it. It just occurs. Now, it is time to give back. I know it and you know it, too. It is time for us to give back to the forces that have shaped us. This is something we will carry with us for the rest of our lives."

"Do we need to take anything?" Karla asked.

"What would we take? All we have is within us."

PART TWO:
TO THE PAST

TO THE PAST

I took one simple step
A choice, a move, a risk
That drifted into mist
And grew from sphere to sphere.

Inside, I sensed the Earth.
All parts at once a world. Wet,
In Spring. Warm,
In Summer. Willing,
In Autumn. Wanting,
In Winter.

Four corners, four seasons
Two persons, two reasons.
One space in the past
A place that will last,
Forever.

Cynthia Marigold

CHAPTER THREE

A SLIP IN TIME

When they crossed the bridge from St. Joseph to Benton Harbor, Karla wondered if they could possibly accomplish this mysterious rescue based solely upon Cynthia's vision. Cynthia seemed so sure of herself, and the cause so worthwhile, yet Karla was filled with apprehension. She had the sensation of being back inside the fish bowl without the hangover.

Karla sat in Cynthia's car and felt herself removed from the quiet scenes of Benton Harbor that she viewed, absently, through the windshield. People hurried in the cold morning air of the midwestern, mostly middle-class, hard-working city to their jobs and their errands. Karla surmised that completing last minute Christmas details was a primary motivation for the silent rush outside the windshield. Reasonable enough. She should be attending to the same mundane tasks. Yet, here she was, riding slowly along snowy streets, sitting beside eccentric, optimistic Cynthia Marigold looking for a time slip in which to travel to the winter of 1895, to become a part of two women she wasn't even sure existed.

Karla did not know what to expect. She glanced at Cynthia who was hunched over the steering wheel staring with blazing determination into the middle distance. Maybe if the people outside stopped and waved, cheering them on in their mission of mercy Karla could have mustered a greater sense of purpose.

What do I expect, Karla thought? Maybe bright white lights announcing the time slip like a neon billboard at the roadside? The Hallelujah Chorus? The sheer idiocy of her thoughts prevented Karla from laughing out loud.

She remembered feeling much the same years ago, when Cynthia had offered to test her biological age. Then, as now, a

16

sensation of fear mixed with interest had surfaced within her. It was a warning mixed with a curious desire, like the first time she had been sexually aroused. What might be revealed that she did not already know? What secrets of her behavior might rise from the subconscious spaces under her skin? A much younger Cynthia had stood ready then, smiling, enthusiastic, encouraging; then, as now, suggesting that to segue from here to there might contain an element of insight if she was open to the experience.

Cynthia pulled the car into a gravel driveway and drove slowly through an opening between two rundown warehouses to the edge of the ship canal. One building had a "for rent" sign tacked to the wall facing Main Street. The other had an equally abandoned look. Shards of glass from broken windows glinted on the ground, their jagged shapes part of the hopelessness of the litter and debris that were strewn among the weeds growing next to the forgotten canal.

Karla knew that the ship canal had been designed in 1860 by a civil engineer named J.E. Miller. If memory served her, Miller had been associated with Martin Green in a dredging and contracting business. Their offices had been located on North Wells Street in downtown Chicago.

As much as times had changed, many things remained the same. Benton Harbor leaders of today appealed to Chicago businesses for exchange of commerce. More than a century ago, at the urging of Sterne Brunson, one of Benton Harbor's early presidents, Miller and Green had been approached to design and dredge the ship canal.

Karla remembered reading that Brunson had traveled from Benton Harbor to Chicago by boat with two other businessmen, Henry Morton and Charles Hull. Their purpose was to secure water access from Benton Harbor to Lake Michigan. It sounded so similar to the commercial passenger ships that Benton Harbor was currently negotiating for with a firm in Chicago.

As long ago as 1860, Sterne Brunson's vision had made today's business possible. His proposed ship canal would run nearly a mile from the St. Joseph River to downtown Benton Harbor. It would contain a basin broad enough to accommodate the largest commercial steamers. The steamers would bring

17

business and industry to Benton Harbor.

After much discussion, Miller and Green agreed to inspect the proposed site of the project. They made what would be the first of many lake crossings on a small round-bottomed propeller vessel.

Looking at the old ship canal, Karla wondered what those men had seen. Before the development, the entire area had been a marsh.

Cynthia stopped the car in an open space between the rental and the canal. She stroked the smooth skin of her jaw and stared straight ahead, leaning forward on the seat, looking for something that would be visible only to them.

Cynthia released her grip on the steering wheel long enough to rub nervously along the angular bone of her jaw. The familiar gesture was not lost on Karla. She's scared, too, Karla thought, feeling somewhat better with the knowledge that hers was not the only fear.

Karla scanned the deserted site and fervently hoped that no one else was here on this bitter winter morning. She shuddered to think what type of individual might be lurking around an abandoned ship canal in the dead of winter. Images of bag men and muggers marched ominously through her mind. Armed and unannounced, criminals hid within her mental crevices waiting for unsuspecting passersby. Karla shook off her nervous thoughts and looked around.

Behind the decrepit warehouses, the little used shipping canal formed a dugout artery to what had once been Benton Harbor's center, its beginning, its heart.

Ducks, rails and cranes still populated the wetlands bordering the St. Joseph and Paw Paw Rivers. Wild rice still grew in the remaining marsh, though Karla knew that it was not as prolific as it had been in the early years.

When Miller and Green agreed to undertake the dredging, the birds, turtles and muskrats had moved farther up the Paw Paw River. The men had decided that the canal should be 150 feet wide to enable the bulky lake vessels to turn. It did not appear to be that wide now. Karla estimated the canal to be about 80 feet at most. What had happened to their original design? Government intervention? Lack of funds?

Cynthia shoved her purse underneath the front seat and cranked up the car's heater. Absorbed in thoughts of her own, Cynthia sat back and stared ahead.

Enormous steamers had once moored up to the pilings that now stood broken and dulled, their rotting remains jutting from under the still water's surface providing an unfettered nesting place for pond scum.

Benton Harbor had been a major commercial shipping port until overland trucking had squeezed the life out of the industry. In the early days, the turning basin had formed a wide triangle of water at the east end of the canal where Pipestone Avenue crossed Main Street.

Sterne Brunson lived on the bluff nearest to the basin. At the eastern side, on a hill, lived Henry C. Morton. Still farther east sat the home of Charles Hull. They had probably gathered in Brunson's parlor and mulled over the dredging project.

Sand from the swampy bottom had been used to fill in the banks of the canal. It made a firm foundation for the docks and platforms that were constructed there. Karla pressed her lips together as she thought about those simpler times. Dredging today was an annual problem for both cities. Governmental regulations made the disposal of the dredged sand next to impossible now.

Cynthia glanced at Karla and pulled again on the smooth skin along her jaw. "It's around here somewhere . . . we'll know it when we see it," Cynthia said opening the car door.

"At that rate, you'll wear out your face before you're forty." Karla said in an attempt to sound lighthearted.

"Ha, ha." Cynthia said. But, she made a conscious effort to remove her hand from her face.

"Do you want to lock it?"

"What?"

"The car. Do you want to lock it?"

"No need, we'll only be gone from the present for a few seconds. That is, if I can locate the damn thing." Cynthia continued to look earnestly for the time slip. Her blue eyes widened, searched and focused like careful spotlights as she scanned the area.

19

A few seconds. We'll only be gone from the present for a few seconds. Karla swallowed the lump in her throat and felt it rise immediately back into position. She checked her watch: 9:20 a.m. She should be opening the store in ten minutes. It was the Christmas countdown. Maggie would need her. Doily might be out of cat food. Maybe she should just leave now. The keys were in the ignition. Cynthia would understand.

"It's here!" Cynthia exclaimed, jumping up with a sudden, graceful motion that made the jagged layers of her blonde hair stand out from her head. Cynthia ran to a place on the bank of the canal. Temporarily forgetting her fear, Karla hurried to Cynthia's side.

She squinted in awe at the time slip. Reflected in the brightness of the winter morning sun, it looked like the raw edges of an oyster curling underwater in a freely formed oval with no beginning and no end. The entrance to its center — a pale brown passage the color of heavy cream in coffee — also had no apparent end although it most certainly did begin right there on the banks of the canal. Karla felt weak and exhilarated in the same instant. Blood rushed to her fingertips, pounding into each extremity like tiny vessels pushed by heartbeats that pulsated so purposefully, so desperately to the ends of her fingers, Karla thought they might explode in ten furious directions. She swallowed hard on the persistent lump in her throat and tried again to think of a way to back out of this crazy adventure.

A pregnant image of Doreen crowded into her mind. Doreen who had one baby after another and never seemed to grow past the old points of sarcasm, jealousy and dissatisfaction. Karla would surely need assistance from another place in time to make peace with her sister. Could she deny the power within herself to help others? She had that chance right now.

The creamy, beige inside of the slip flowed smoothly into itself, lit from within by a translucent shimmer that gave it the quality of mother-of-pearl or drops of oil on water. It reminded Karla of coffee the way she liked it in the morning: beige, she always said. To which, people often replied "oh, you like a little coffee with your cream." The memory provided a moment of comfortable warmth and the insistent pulse stopped pushing so

20

hard on the skin of her fingertips.

Cynthia had selected four smooth stones from the canal bank and stood quietly holding two of the thick stones in each of her open palms. She recited a soft chant that was unfamiliar to Karla. Knowing Cynthia, she was probably making it up as she went along, Karla thought. Cynthia's eyes were closed and her sturdy body was framed with an aura of glowing pale light that extended along her outstretched arms and covered the open stretch of her fingers like radiant gloves.

Viewing her friend, Karla relaxed. She felt her fear turn to admiration and trust. This was the woman of health and wellness, a reader of people, her counselor and confidant. Cynthia's receptiveness to new ideas, spiritual challenges, her kindness and morality had expanded Karla's own vision on countless occasions. Her trust in Cynthia had developed gradually as she had witnessed her conscious approach to living. Cynthia believed that everything happened purposefully. She carefully studied the signposts in her life, learning from the messages presented, adjusting and accepting as she went along.

Karla remembered the first time Cynthia had shared her belief in purpose. Years ago, Karla had decided to give up on Doreen, to stop the constant bickering by avoiding her sister completely, by writing Doreen out of her life. Cynthia had said no, keep trying, your sister has a purpose in your life, she was chosen for you for a reason, and you were chosen for her. You may never understand what that reason is, Cynthia had said, but you owe it to yourself to keep trying. She is your sister.

Now, Cynthia's aura moved around her like a warm beacon of light. It was so bright, so prevalent, that Karla was constantly amazed that other people could not see it. As auras went — for Karla, at least — Cynthia's was impossible to miss. Like Cynthia, it fairly bounced in place.

Mesmerized by the ethereal lights of the slip now clearly defined on the banks, Karla moved toward Cynthia and listened to the steady rhythm of her chant:

Lapping water
ripples on the wind

from the north, the south,
the east, the west.

Lapping water
cream carpet of mirth
ripples in the wind
from sunlit sky, blue Mother Earth.

Lapping water
ripples with the wind
gently overlapping
from the present to the past.

She accepted Cynthia's outstretched hand and felt a powerful surge of energy at the touch. Cynthia swept the air with her left hand and pressed two of the canal stones into Karla's palm, securing them in place as she covered Karla's hand with her own. Together, with one simple step, they slipped through the wavy edges of the passageway and drifted into the slip's creamy smoothness that immediately enveloped them like a warm mist on a summer day.

Pervasive within the slip was a clean damp smell, like wet earth in spring . . . a sprinkled summer garden . . . mown grass in autumn or the first breath of snow on a marsh. Its odor was of all parts of the earth connecting to all parts of the universe. It was a composite of every season, every person, every place and all directions.

❦ **Chapter Four**

THE HEALING RITUAL

At first, Karla was unaware of their transformation. As they meshed with the shimmering mist within the slip, Cynthia released her hand and Karla was left holding the two stones that Cynthia had pressed into her palm when they entered. Cynthia held the remaining two. Both women stood on the canal bank with palms outstretched to the evening sky. Karla squinted in the moonlight. All four stones — previously thick and whole — now contained worn holes in their centers as if something gradual and persistent like lapping water or nudging wind had licked through their hard surfaces.

She stood very still. Her breath came out in moist puffs that appeared and disappeared in the blackness. It was late, they had passed from morning into night, from the present to the past, from the known to the unknown. Yet Karla felt safe. In the present she would never have ventured to this place after dark. Now, she had a sense of stability and security in these surroundings.

The great ship canal was intact. Sturdy pilings wrapped with rope supported vast shipping and receiving platforms. Ice floes formed deep circles where the pilings met the water. A lone drake, roused from a floating sleep, quacked from beneath the docks.

Karla slipped the stones into the tiny purse she was carrying and noticed the scratchy texture of raw silk against her bare hand. Finding a pair of woven mittens inside the purse, she put them on. The dress she was wearing covered her high-buttoned shoes and she wore a heavy, street length woolen coat with a woolly collar. A tam — perfectly matched to the coat — was precariously perched upon the coiled bun of brown hair pinned securely to the crown of her head. Karla straightened the tam and smoothed tendrils of the long hair that now framed her face. It felt soft and familiar. She dug inside the purse for a hand mirror.

Karla absorbed her changed attire as if it was the most normal thing in the world, which indeed it was, for a resident of Benton Harbor in 1895. The woman standing beside her — Karla knew with certainty — was not Cynthia Marigold, albeit their smooth faces were identical, but Dr. Theodora Goodhart.

Cynthia's short and shaggy blonde hair, emphasized by three pierced earrings in her right ear, was gone. In its place was a long flow of blonde hair wrapped in a soft braid and pinned, just slightly off-center, to the top of Theodora's head. She wore a street length plaid coat with a turned-up collar and held a worn black leather doctor's bag in her right hand. Her left hand held two smooth stones with holes in their center. She was staring down at the stones.

Feeling Karla's eyes on her face, Dr. Theodora Goodhart looked up.

"Hello, Grace," Theodora said tentatively. The words rose on puffs of breath that appeared like tiny clouds in the cold night air. "Grace Shepard . . . your name, I have always thought, has a decidedly gentle ring to it, but you look so very distressed this evening. May I offer my assistance?"

Karla listened to the proper syntax which projected easily from the lips that belonged to Cynthia Marigold and felt an urge to touch the smooth skin on the concerned face of the woman doctor standing before her. However, Karla knew, a familiar gesture such as that would be highly unacceptable in 1895, even between good friends. Grace Shepard's influence on Karla Cifelli clearly indicated the use of polite restraint.

A horse whinnied nearby. Hooves scuffled restlessly on the snow covered gravel and a carriage creaked with the movement. Grace glanced back at her horse and made an over-sized hand gesture that the animal understood. Karla stared at her hand — the hand that she now shared with Grace Shepard — in amazement as the horse stood still, waiting for her mistress.

"Thank you, Theodora. I am so relieved to locate you. For some reason, I have no idea why, I knew to look for you here. Somehow, I was certain you would be here," Grace Shepard said. She breathed a quick sigh of relief. Her face was flushed to a rosy hue in the cold winter air.

Karla Cifelli and Grace Shepard were identical. Both women favored a demeanor which was void of the make-up which might have been employed to cover the lightly freckled nose and too rosy cheeks.

Grace Shepard turned to Theodora and said, "Susan, my youngest, is very ill. Will you come?"

"Might she have consumption? Cases of it have been persisting all through October and November . . ."

"We thought so at first," Grace replied. "Helen had quinine in the house and we administered that. But it seemed to have no effect."

"Does she have the chills?"

Grace nodded. "And a high fever."

"How long has she been down?"

"Three days."

"Hm-m . . ." Theodora mused. "Consumption normally takes twenty-four hours to run its course. But in one so young . . ."

"Susan is also very thin. Even with Helen's excellent cooking, we have been unsuccessful in tempting her to eat much of anything."

As they climbed aboard one of the Shepard's winter carriages, Grace surveyed the peaceful scene at the shipping canal. She knew instinctively why a busy professional like her friend Dr. Theodora Goodhart would choose to walk here on her way home from a call. The vast docks with their huge pilings bound with immense rope were beginning to freeze into the waters fed by the St. Joseph and the Paw Paw Rivers. Muted echoes of cracking ice and wind in the bare trees bounced off of the walls and into the empty spaces. The wide, heavy platforms built of thick planks exuded an illusion of such permanence, Grace could scarcely fathom the dilapidated scene she now knew existed for this place.

The desperate image of the future with its rotting pilings and stagnant water vanished like a whisper as Grace Shepard lightly flicked the reins and her horse trotted gaily through the snow turning east onto Main Street from the docks.

"The pavement affords a smoother ride . . ." Theodora commented as the carriage left the gravel and turned onto the paving bricks of Main Street. She let the sentence end without finishing it.

Grace nodded agreeably. Cynthia Marigold also had the habit of letting sentences wander and the old familiarity comforted the part of Karla Cifelli that was present inside the body of Grace Shepard. At least some of their traits had passed with them through the time slip, Karla thought. She wondered how much of a contribution two women would be allowed to make in Victorian 1895.

Grace said, "I believe Benton Harbor is making excellent progress and it is good to hear your positive comment. There are so many who criticized the notion of paving this roadway."

"People are afraid of change. In time, they will remember it as their idea . . ."

"Yes, I have noticed that phenomenon before, foibles of human nature."

"Exactly. I have no inclination whatsoever why people, in general of course, insist upon making their lives so very difficult with negative talk."

"Others long to hear it, I suppose," Grace replied. "They say that bad news travels twice as fast as good. I believe that most people want to think that the lives and actions of others are worse than their own."

"If people would only realize their own power. Positive actions are so much more effective than negative. Why, if everyone would commit to performing just one kind deed each day the state of the world would be much improved."

"That is true, Theodora," Grace said. Then, whispered, "Do you suppose that is what it will take with us?"

"I have no idea. No idea at all. I only know that Cynthia Marigold and Karla Cifelli were called upon from another place in time to help us here and now. What that means to us exactly, I do not know. But it feels right to me."

"To me, too."

"You know, Grace, people in the future will spend years in therapy trying to get in touch with their feelings. You and I are ahead of our time, and so are Cynthia and Karla. Acting upon intuitions will always be a risky business, but it is what makes dreams into realities."

Grace held the reins as Belle led the way through downtown Benton Harbor past the prosperous businesses that had made the city's population increase by more than 5,000 in the thirty-five years since the ship canal was installed.

Located just sixty miles from Chicago by steam ship, Benton Harbor had become a popular resort destination as well as an important commercial shipping port. Fresh produce, flour, lumber and furs were loaded for delivery to the big cities before transporting passengers back for pastoral visits to rural Benton Harbor.

As the agricultural industry boomed, hundreds of families had traveled from New York and other seaboard states to settle east of the St. Joseph river. Benton Harbor had grown into a thriving city of beautiful homes. Modern Queen Anne, Italianate and up-dated Greek Revival structures nestled into neat landscapes planted with orchards and field crops.

It was the ship canal that had enabled Benton Harbor's rapid, early expansion. Before the canal, pioneers had settled west of the St. Joseph River and the small peninsula of land called St. Joseph had soon become densely populated with no room for additional growth. Limited land in St. Joseph between the shores of Lake Michigan and the river had forced new settlers inland, across the river to the east where land was plentiful and affordable. When access to Lake Michigan and markets across the water had presented an immediate challenge to growers and landowners, digging a shipping canal — arduous work for crews in the 1860s — had solved the problem, enabling the unprecedented population boom in the fertile region.

Grace was uncertain whether she guided the reins or if Belle turned automatically onto Sixth Street and then east again onto Territorial Road. Grace noticed the newly installed electric lights of the Yore Opera House burning inside as they passed by the huge corner building. Personally, she held the opinion that electricity was quite unnecessary, as did many others, which made the invention rather controversial. But, all of that aside, Grace wondered who might be working at this late hour.

Theodora pulled the collar of her coat more closely around

her neck and held it there. The December air was bitterly cold with the west wind blowing off of Lake Michigan. The effort to keep warm forced them both to shrink down into their heavy coats and pull the fur throw Grace kept in the carriage more snugly around their knees. Grace had placed a warming pot on the floorboards between their feet, but the coals had long since lost their heat.

"I hear many positive comments about your practice, Theodora," Grace said. "People say you have the gift of healing."

"I hope it will extend to your daughter."

Yes, I pray that it will, Grace thought as she turned into the driveway of her home. The Shepard house was located on the eastern edge of Benton Harbor up on a hill near the Morton farm just off of Territorial Road. Gas lights glowed through stained glass windows in the lower level and one dim light burned in an upstairs bedroom where little Susan Shepard lay weak and delirious with the fever.

They were met at the side door by Grace's husband, Dan, and his mother Helen. Dan took the reins from Grace and led Belle out to the barn.

"Welcome to our home, Dr. Goodhart," Helen Shepard said. She embraced Theodora and took the heavy coat and scarf, hanging them on hooks near the entry. "Susan is unable even to sip a little water. She is burning up with the fever."

"And the other children?" Theodora asked.

"My son took them across the road to Martha Bennett's."

The older woman led the way through the outside entry to an inner hallway where a narrow, maple staircase ascended to the second floor. The women climbed in single file to the child's bedroom.

Grace's heart raced when she saw her little girl lying still beneath a velvet patchwork quilt. She moved to the bed's far side and bent to caress the child's cheek. It was hot to the touch. Grace stepped back in deference to Theodora who had pulled back the quilt and begun examining Susan's tiny arms and chest. Her fragile body barely stirred with her shallow breathing. Grace stood still watching the delicate rise and fall of her daughter's small body. She looked so helpless lying there, just as she had six years ago when Grace had given birth to her in the bedroom downstairs. Then, Grace remembered, she had been overwhelmed with the sensation that this little baby had been given to her to love and care for, to bathe and feed and dress and educate. She had held the new baby and wondered if she would be capable of the countless responsibilities of child rearing. What if the child was injured, or became ill? Would she know what to do? Grace had feared then that she might not be strong enough to live with her anxieties. And what of the many questions the child was certain to ask? Would she have the answers? Grace had held her beautiful baby to her breast and wept. She wanted to do that now, but she blinked back the tears she felt welling up behind her eyes and stood stoically, waiting.

"Please bring up a bowl of cool water and a wash cloth," Theodora said, opening her bag, "and a pot of hot water for the medicines."

Both Grace and Helen moved instantly toward the door. As they walked through the unusually large parlor that Helen's father-in-law had built for his growing family Grace asked, "Has there been any change at all since I left?"

"She has not so much as opened her eyes," Helen replied in a fretful tone. "She has not stirred or asked for a thing. The fever can be so contagious, I am afraid for all of us. Martha will keep the other children as long as necessary, but Dan said she fears for the health of her own children."

"Yes, I spoke with her this morning," Grace said. "This house seems so quiet without them, even when they are sleeping the house feels alive with their presence. I miss them. When did Dan return?"

"About an hour before you did," Helen answered. She poured water into a basin.

Grace added a log to the stove and put a kettle of fresh water on the top to boil. She retrieved towels, wash cloths and fresh sheets for Susan's bed from the pantry. When she selected one of Susan's cotton nightgowns from a pile on the shelf the pervading sense of the child's fragile helplessness overtook her and Grace began to weep.

Helen came to her side and Grace allowed herself only a

29

moment of sorrow in the presence of her mother-in-law.

Swallowing with a visible effort, Grace dried her tears and stood up straight with determination. "I am sorry Mother Helen," Grace said. "I must be strong for Susan's sake, for all of our sakes. Dr. Goodhart will need my help to prepare her medicines."

Dan returned from the barn then and Grace turned her head away to prevent him from seeing her reddened face. She quickly bent over a basin on a washstand near the pantry and splashed her skin with icy water. She had seen the grave expression on his face when she returned with Theodora. She knew that Dan was not strong where his children were concerned. She did not wish to add to his worries.

Grace and Helen carried the items Theodora had requested up the stairs and into the tiny, simple bedroom Susan shared with her sister. Minuscule by any standards, the white-washed room contained two small beds with a lamp on a table between them, one armoire and a slatted wooden rocker. A single window overlooked the orchards. Following the custom of the day, the Shepards had not lavished any expense on furnishing their children's sleeping quarters.

"She will need regular sponge baths to break the fever," Theodora said looking up from the medicines she was grinding with a pestle and mortar on her lap. Dr. Theodora Goodhart was well-known in Benton Harbor and St. Joseph for adhering to some of the older medicinal techniques which she expertly combined with more modern ones.

Taking charge of the situation with gentle authority, Theodora said, "Grace, you and I will take turns with the baths. Good, you brought fresh linens, frequent changes will be necessary. Mrs. Shepard, you look very tired. I advise you to get some rest, Grace and I can attend to Susan."

"Will she be all right?" Helen Shepard asked. She squeezed her hands so tightly together that her knuckles turned white. "Will you make her well?"

"I honestly cannot say at this juncture. The fever is very high and she does not seem able to swallow," Theodora said, dipping a sponge into the bowl and wringing out the excess water. She gently blotted Susan's forehead. "She is so thin, there is very little reserve strength to draw upon. I will try my best, Mrs. Shepard."

"I pray that you will succeed, Dr. Goodhart. And when you do, I shall make it my personal mission to see that this child grows plump and healthy." Helen Shepard's optimistic words were overshadowed by the doubting tone in her voice. As she turned and left the room, the concern on her face hardened into a grim acceptance of death.

Theodora placed some of the powdered medicines into a small marble bowl which she carried in her bag. She carefully poured a portion of the hot water into the bowl and covered it with a cloth. Grace observed the process with interest. Dr. Bell simply called for medications from the druggist. Theodora was different, her methods were less patent, more personal and — in Grace's estimation — more suitable to cure an individual patient.

Together they patted Susan's arms, legs and chest with the damp sponge and changed the bed linens and Susan's night-gown. They alternated administering the baths and attempting to spoon small amounts of water, the medicine and warm chicken broth into Susan's mouth. Yet, the child did not respond.

"She is not taking enough liquid," Theodora said, placing a cool wash cloth on Susan's forehead. "Her body feels cooler to the touch but I am concerned about dehydration. Will you prepare a bowl of ice chips? We can try melting those on her tongue."

Grace hurried downstairs. In her haste, she could not locate the ice pick. Finding a heavy knife, she broke off a chunk of ice from the block in the icebox and pummeled it into chips. The process seemed to take forever until, finally, Grace rushed back upstairs with a bowl of the melting chips.

At ten minutes to midnight, Theodora gently shook Grace's shoulder. Grace started abruptly from the rocker at the foot of Susan's bed where she had fallen asleep. An expression of anxiety washed across her pale face. She had been dreaming of Susan as a baby, such an easy child, a tiny quiet baby who nursed at her breast and rarely cried. Grace doubted if she could withstand the pain of the death of this child, the baby she had raised for six years. She regarded Theodora with wide eyes and opened her mouth to speak.

"Sh-sh-sh," Theodora whispered putting a finger to her lips.

"Everyone is asleep. We must perform a ritual of healing that will cast a circle of protection around Susan. I have exhausted every other avenue. I hope you do not mind, but while you slept, I collected everything we will need from your kitchen."

Grace did not understand, but she did not protest. Her daughter was still alive and insuring her health was all that mattered to Grace. She rose quietly from the rocker and splashed the sleep from her face with water from the basin.

A blue cotton cloth that Grace recognized as a table cover was spread over Susan's tiny body. A candle on the nightstand cast a bluish light over Susan's fragile face.

Grace stood next to Theodora as she lit a stick of dried sage leaves wrapped with string. Theodora invoked a circle of protection around Susan's bed, casting smoke into the four corners of the room, the four directions of the universe. She took extra care at the window blowing smoke into the sash and sill. She moved swiftly, lighting four white candles representing the directions of north, south, east and west. The room was bright with the candlelight and shadows danced in the corners. Theodora instructed Grace to breathe deeply and to visualize the sickly child in good health, running and playing under a clear, blue sky.

When a flow of energy was established between them, Theodora moved to the nightstand and held both of her hands over a glass of water. Grace continued praying for a healthy, active child; she imagined Susan on Belle's back riding happily through the orchards, picking fruit from the trees. As Theodora bent over and administered a sip of the water to Susan, Grace knelt on the floor and prayed fervently for the full recovery of the child she could not bear to lose. Susan's face glowed with a gentle blue aura reflected from the indigo cloth in the candlelight.

Following Theodora's lead, Grace stood and the women joined hands, reaching to the sky beyond the wooden ceiling. They swayed together, gently rocking from side to side. Pushed rhythmically from within, each woman visualized Susan playing beneath a healing blue sky. Grace opened her eyes and looked at Theodora. With her eyes closed, Theodora was smiling peacefully, the smooth skin of her face glowed in the soft light. Grace glanced down again and felt her eyelashes against her cheeks.

They were wet with tears. A silent prayer for her daughter surfaced in her mind like a night breeze. She squeezed Theodora's hand and murmured "Amen."

Theodora opened the circle and the women knelt down, pressing their open palms flat on the wooden floor. Grace felt a rush of excess energy flowing out through her palms and fingertips to the floorboards below. She stared at her hands pressed flat against the floor. Energy was neither created or destroyed. It simply moved from one form into another.

"Do you think it worked?" Grace asked. She felt completely relaxed, refreshed from the fatigue she had experienced prior to falling asleep in the rocker. She rinsed her hands in the basin, drying them on a linen towel carefully embroidered with the letter *S*.

"The energy was strong as it always will be between us, Grace. We have the deep understanding of true sisters," Theodora answered. She, too, rinsed her hands in the water and dried them on the towel. "Yes, I think the ritual worked. I feel as confident about this one as I ever have — present or future."

She winked at Grace.

Then, Theodora picked up all of the remaining pieces of the healing ritual and gathered them into the blue cotton cloth. She placed the candle drippings, the leftover sage stick and ashes, the glass and the remaining drops of water into the center of the cloth and tied its four corners together into a neat bundle.

"I need to cast these articles into the river," Theodora said. "I can go and be back before the first light. You stay here and get some rest, Susan may awaken and need you.

Grace felt the worry lines leave her face. "Take Belle, she is the most familiar with the river route," she said. "I will wait for you here. And Theodora, thank you, my friend . . . my sister."

When Theodora left, Grace sat down in the old rocker and closed her eyes. She thought of her own mother and the baby she had lost at birth, years before Grace was born. It had been a baby girl. A sister that never existed. Her mother often spoke to Grace of the empty feeling that had lingered in her heart after the child had died. It was a hole that could never be filled, her mother had said. Grace had cried when her mother first spoke of the lost baby; she had wished for the power to fill her mother's void. But that power did not exist, and even in childhood, Grace had understood this. She had become a withdrawn and reserved child as a result. Once, she had overheard her mother telling a neighbor that she was a difficult child to love.

Grace drifted in and out of a restless sleep dreaming of her mother and her baby sister, of the emptiness that could never be filled, of the lost love in her life and her fragile helplessness to remedy the ills of those she cared about. It is no wonder that Karla never had children, Grace thought. It is too hard.

Chapter Five

WE WILL ALWAYS BE HERE

Bright winter sunlight streamed into the upstairs bedroom warming Grace's face in an awakening that was gentle, yet immediately anxious. She shifted in the rocking chair and squinted into the room.

Susan was sitting up in bed playing with her dolls.

"Hi mommy," the little girl said.

Grace could not help herself, she ran to the bed and hugged her daughter, stroking her hair and weeping with joy. The tears she had held back last night now streamed down her cheeks, let out like an open reservoir, wetting Susan's hair, as she held the healthy girl and sobbed.

"What's wrong, Mommy?" Susan asked.

"Wrong? Nothing is wrong, Susan, absolutely nothing," Grace answered, smoothing Susan's hair with the palm of her hand. She gazed into the innocent face of her child and hugged her again, weeping until she felt wrung out of tears.

"Someday, I will explain to you the value of crying when you are happy, Susan. Right now, I just need to do it and to hold you. It feels so good to have you healthy in my arms."

Grace carried Susan downstairs to the kitchen where Helen had a fire going in the stove and another crackling in the fireplace. The kitchen radiated warmth, but cracks in the house's uneven construction kept it from being too stuffy. Fresh air flowed inside the room like a warm breeze.

"Look who is well!" Grace exclaimed, hugging Susan again as she carried her into the kitchen.

"Praise be," Helen said taking the child from Grace. "You hungry, honey?"

Susan nodded shyly. She looked confused.

"You have been very sick," her grandmother said. "We are going to fatten you up and keep you well."

Grace prepared a tray of food and carried it up to Theodora. She sat on the bed next to her friend and reported the events of the morning. Theodora spread jam on a warm biscuit and sipped coffee from a thin porcelain cup and saucer. Despite the long night, Theodora looked rested and contented. Her blue eyes sparkled with purpose.

"Is it time for us to go back?" Grace asked doubtfully. It all seemed too easy.

"Susan is not the one we were sent to help, she just happened to benefit from our being here," Theodora answered in a low voice. "We will just have to wait a little longer and see."

"In truth Theodora, that is a relief, I rather like it here," Grace mused. "It is as if I belong here, as if I have found my niche in time." She felt feminine in the long calico dressing gown she had put on last night. The big house on the hill was solid and comfortable; and she felt a deep respect and longing for her husband.

"In some ways we will always be here . . ." Theodora said letting the words drift away.

Chapter Six

MRS. KATHLEEN CARTER

Dan came in from the orchards and sat down for lunch. His eyes were rimmed in red and it was obvious he had been crying. Grace clearly saw the pale blue aura of light hugging his body, supporting him beyond any human strength.

Grace could not have described this gentle force within her that had the ability to read auras and the power to understand things which were not of this place and time. She felt no need to. She was unafraid of the increased wisdom and the growing confidence that had become a part of her since the person of Karla Cifelli had entered her body.

Grace had been open to Karla from the first moment. She had made room for her as if she were an old friend. Grace could not comprehend how Karla had come to her from the future or how Cynthia Marigold had entered into Dr. Theodora's psyche. But that did not matter. She felt no need for explanations or reassurances. She knew that Karla had become a part of her out of kindness, that both of the women from the future were here to help. The feeling that it was good was enough for Grace. She felt no urge to explain this to anyone. Her family and friends would not understand. How could they? She did not understand the phenomenon herself.

"Bannon's boy, Ethan, died of the fever last night. That is the third child this month," Dan said to Grace. He put his head in his hands and slouched over the worktable. The pale blue light of his aura folded around him and drew Grace to him. She put her arms around her husband and leaned against his back. He felt warm and strong as she embraced him yet she felt a shiver of emotional pain run through his spine.

"Susan is all right," she said to his unspoken question. "Mercifully, her fever broke last night."

He looked up at his wife, his eyes brimming with tears. "She

37

was so sick," he said, "so still, I thought— Where is she?"

He went off to find his daughter and came back into the kitchen carrying the little girl. "This is the finest Christmas present we could have," he said, smiling at Susan. "We have so much to be thankful for. See if Dr. Goodhart will join us for church and for supper afterward, will you Grace?"

When Theodora agreed to stay another night, Grace was relieved. She did not want to let Theodora out of her sight just yet. Susan might need her. More than that, Karla needed to talk with Cynthia privately about their next step.

Grace knew eventually that Theodora would have to return to her own residence in town and she would cope with that when the time came. But for now, Grace was content. Her child was well, thanks to Karla and Cynthia, and Grace looked forward to enjoying the Christmas festivities.

She kept busy that day mending, scrubbing laundry and hanging it on a rack in the kitchen to dry. She filled the woodbox twice for the laundry and a third time to heat water for their baths that evening. Grace was determined that they would attend church freshly bathed and dressed in their Sunday best.

Still, despite the diversion afforded by the hard work and the anticipation of a pleasant evening, Grace felt a nagging sensation that something was very wrong. Something was about to happen. Something dreadful and monumental that would mar Benton Harbor for a long time to come.

She pressed a simple dress for Theodora to borrow for the evening and hummed intentionally to rid her thoughts of the ominous sensation. Grace told herself to focus on the prospect of sharing Christmas Eve with her friends at church, decorating their tiny tabletop tree and eating the festive meal Helen was preparing. But the persistent feeling, like an itch she could not scratch, remained steadfast in her mind.

That evening, Dan hitched up their strongest team to a covered leather carriage. He helped Grace into the seat next to his, kissing her lightly on the lips as he did so. She blushed and, out of habit, glanced quickly around. Normally, she was embarrassed at any public display of affection. But tonight Grace found that she did not truly care what other people thought. She had more important issues on her mind.

"Something is wrong," she had whispered to Theodora as they walked to the barn.

"I know," Theodora had replied. "I can feel it, too."

Theodora and Helen sat in the second seat with their legs covered with heavy lap robes and their hands thrust snugly inside fur-lined muffs. Grace had made the woolen dresses that she and Theodora were wearing. She had pinned a cameo brooch once belonging to her grandmother to the center of the high lace collar on her dress. Her hair was wrapped in a loose coil on the crown of her head.

Theodora wore an amber pendant around her neck that had also belonged to Grace's grandmother. Grace had insisted that Theodora wear it to set off her blond hair. Both women were wrapped in embroidered cloaks which had belonged to Helen's mother.

"Are you warm enough, Mother Helen?" Grace said, turning in her seat.

"Yes, thank you." Helen replied. "Are you quite warm, Dr. Theo?"

Theodora nodded affirmatively and smiled, but Grace could see that the aura around her body was jagged and troubled.

Young Danny drove his six brothers and sisters in the large family carriage behind the adults. Grace could hear them singing Christmas carols above the familiar sounds of the horses hooves clomping over the snow-covered dirt road. Graceful oak trees grew along the shoulders and blended easily with the old orchards of peach and apricot trees. Grace could almost smell their fragrance, so strong was her memory of the annual harvest time. Yet, the peace and comfort of her memories and of having her family and good friend with her were not enough to dispel the foreboding that remained uppermost in her mind.

Now, as they drove toward the Benton Harbor Methodist Church, Grace attempted again to direct her thoughts to the spiritual aspects of the season. Thin strains of the children singing "Silent Night" and "The First Noel" drifted over the clatter of the carriages on the bumpy roadway.

Grace began humming one of the familiar tunes, but before

she had completed two measures, the carol was interrupted by the high-pitched voice of a female screaming and a carriage careening toward theirs at breakneck speed. Dan quickly pulled their team over to the shoulder of the narrow dirt road and shouted back at young Danny to do the same with the children's carriage.

"Mr. Shepard, please stop!" Emily Carter called as she pulled her horse to a jerky halt next to the Shepard carriage. She was not wearing a hat and the long curls of her hair flew wildly about her face.

"Oh, Dr. Goodhart, you are here!" Emily continued shouting with an edge of panic in her voice. "I have been to your office and I was driving out to the Shepard place in the fervent hope that you would be there. Mother is feeling so poorly and she refuses to see anyone but you. She keeps repeating 'find Dr. Theo, find Dr. Theo,' and I have been desperately trying to find you for two whole days. Please, will you come?"

Without hesitation, Theodora assured the anxious girl that she would come at once. She leaned to the front of the carriage and said, "Grace, I sincerely loath asking this of you on Christmas Eve, but Miss Emily is in a state of shock. If I need any help with Mrs. Carter, she will be useless to assist me. Would you mind terribly coming along?"

Grace looked at Dan. "Go along Grace," he said. "We have so much to be thankful for, it is time to share with others. Be safe and return home as soon as you are able."

Theodora and Grace sat in the second seat of Emily's expensive carriage and clung tightly onto the sideboards as Emily whipped her horse into a gallop. The horse obliged as best as he could. Steam rose in a mist from the horse's lathered back and his hooves slipped on several of the snowy inclines in the bumpy road. As the carriage rattled noisily over potholes, Grace felt as though her teeth might jar out of her head.

Emily Carter lived with her mother Kathleen in a sprawling Queen Anne mansion on the southern end of town. It was easily one of the largest homes in Benton Harbor and there was considerable speculation among the townspeople as to how Kathleen Carter could afford such a modern house. As far as anyone in

40

Benton Harbor knew, there had never been a Mr. Carter.

Kathleen herself was one of the leading actresses at the Yore Opera House and received a modest income for her work there. Fifteen-year-old Emily worked part-time at the opera house's box office. Neither salary could account for the acquisition or furnishing of their enormous living quarters.

Emily jerked the lathered horse to an abrupt halt at the front entrance and spoke breathlessly. "Please go right in, Mother is in the front bedroom at the top of the stairs. I will take care of Buster and be in as soon as I can."

The path had not been cleared and the front of the manse was dark. In the moonlight, Grace recognized the shadowy forms of chairs and tables left carelessly out on the porch. Like the walkway, the furniture was drifted over with snow, giving the wide circular porch a ghostly air.

Theodora entered the foyer which was illuminated by a single bulb hanging from a wire. The bare light was a tribute to the technology of the day and Kathleen Carter displayed it proudly, sometimes leaving the electricity to burn even in daylight hours. After the Yore Opera House, Kathleen Carter had been among the first in Benton Harbor to have electric lights, and the bare bulb, harsh and unnecessary as it appeared to Grace, was meant to display Kathleen Carter's fancy lifestyle to everyone who entered.

A carved mahogany staircase made its way into a parlor which was crowded with overstuffed furniture. Red velvet chairs and sofas were pressed against the walls. Ornate wooden tables were wedged between them. Pretentious arrangements of potpourri in flowered bowls, scented candles and knick-knacks of every type covered the tabletops. Draperies sewn from heavy green velvet hung in thick folds from somber valances at the windows. The effect was of too much furniture in too little space despite the immense size of the room.

Grace stumbled on the layers of plush carpets that Kathleen had piled one on top of another in a needlessly decadent fashion. Grace had heard the neighbor's tongues wagging about the ostentatious waste in Kathleen Carter's home. She disapproved of gossip and resolved not to reveal what she viewed this evening to anyone.

41

Now, as they climbed the stairs to the second story bedroom, Theodora pulled on another chain hanging from a stark light bulb and a life-size painting of Kathleen Carter loomed into view. In the painting she appeared young and beautiful. The artist had highlighted her cheeks to a rosy hue and her rounded breasts pushed at the bodice of the red velvet gown which fell in a swirl at her feet.

"My goodness, Theodora, this is not the Mrs. Carter I remember seeing on the stage," Grace said, staring at the painting.

"Yes, this does appear to be a much younger version."

Kathleen Carter was a small, malnourished looking woman who smoked cigarettes much to the chagrin of Benton Harbor's genteel society members. She wore make-up that always made her appear ready to take the stage even in the daytime. Her brown hair was fringed around her face and she frequently let it hang loosely down her back in direct contrast to the style of the day which dictated that hair be combed closely and conservatively to the head or wrapped tightly in a hairnet. Kathleen's voice was shrill and loud and her aggressive behavior had offended most of the people in Benton Harbor, including many of those who worked with her at the opera house.

When Grace and Theodora entered the open bedroom door at the top of the stairs, Grace gasped audibly. The fabric suspended from the tester over Kathleen's bed was tied to a poster at its foot, exposing Kathleen's face on the pillow. Her skin was shiny with bruises and her lip was swollen to twice its normal size. She gazed through blackened eyelids toward the door.

"Mrs. Carter, who did this to you?" Theodora asked. She advanced to the bedside and, leaning in over the high, narrow bed, took Kathleen's tiny hand in hers. It, too, was cut and bruised as if she had fought and lost with whomever had harmed her.

Theodora put Kathleen's hand gently back on top of the embroidered coverlet and opened her leather doctor's bag. She extracted a flask of whiskey from among the vials in the bag and poured a small amount into one of the water glasses Kathleen kept on a silver tray next to her bed. Theodora gently raised Kathleen's head and held the glass to her lips.

42

Grace sat at a table with four tapestried chairs in the over-sized bedroom while Theodora made a careful examination of her battered patient. This room, too, was cluttered with elaborate furniture some of which Grace recognized as artifacts from stage productions. Dozens of photographs in jeweled and gilded frames depicted Kathleen wearing costumes from past shows. In all of them her hair and make-up were exaggerated, yet immaculate. In comparison with Kathleen's notorious public image, it was alarming to see her lying in her bed, bruised and devoid of the usual adornments of heavy make-up and fancy hairstyles.

Grace remembered when Kathleen Carter and her then two-year-old daughter had arrived in Benton Harbor. They had traveled by coach on the Territorial Road from Detroit with all of their possessions in two carpet bags and a steamer trunk. Emily had cried a lot in those early days and Kathleen often appeared pale and haggard. Kathleen was barely five feet tall and had the scrawny shape of an adolescent. No one seemed to know her and she was not forthcoming with any details of why she had come to Benton Harbor without a husband or any relatives beside Emily. Those facts had not changed in the thirteen years they had re-sided here. No one really knew anything about Kathleen Carter's personal life and now she was lying bruised in her bed and she would not reveal who had done it to her or why.

Emily hurried in and stared anxiously at her mother and Theodora. She was obviously worried yet she remained standing just inside the door and uttered not a word. Grace's heart went out to the young girl. She put her arm around Emily's shoulder and guided her to one of the comfortable chairs near the table.

Emily kept her eyes fixed on her mother. Emily was a stocky girl, tall and healthy looking, strong where Kathleen was fragile. The father must have been a large man, Grace thought, Emily certainly did not take after Kathleen in her physical appearance.

"Miss Emily," Theodora said, "how long has your mother been ailing in this fashion?"

"Two days. I was at the opera house cleaning up after the last show. When I came home, she was lying at the foot of the stairs." Emily began to cry, but she struggled to compose herself and continued with her story, "I helped her get into bed and set off to find you. She refused to see anyone else. When I was unable to locate you, I tried in vain to convince her to enter Westcott's Sanitarium for the cure. She simply would not go, Dr. Theo. She did allow me to give her a hot bath, you know she has a private tub." Despite the worry that was clearly evident in her voice, Emily said the last with a note of pride. Private bathtubs — especially those with hot and cold running water — were very rare in Benton Harbor in 1895. Like the lightbulbs, ostentatious displays of bathtubs served as overt symbols of Victorian wealth.

"You did very well, Miss Emily. Did she say anything to you about what happened?"

"She said she fell down the stairs."

Theodora finished bandaging Kathleen's arm. "Your mother will be fine, young lady," Theodora said producing a brown glass bottle and a spoon from her bag and looking up at Emily with a capable smile. She turned her attention back to Kathleen. "This will help you take your rest. When you are feeling up to it, taking the baths will be beneficial for your muscle aches."

"I will Dr. Theo, later," Kathleen said managing a haughty tone in spite of her aches and pains. "And Dr. Theo? I would appreciate it if you and Mrs. Shepard would keep what you have seen tonight in the utmost confidence. I most certainly do not wish to attract the useless pity of anyone in this town."

Grace thought again of Kathleen's arrival in Benton Harbor thirteen years ago. She had immediately gone to work at the opera house. At first her jobs were housekeeping and box office work in exchange for small but adequate living quarters near the larger and more elaborate dressing rooms.

Then, almost overnight, she began to appear in stage roles that became bigger and better as each season progressed. With her stage successes, Kathleen lost her anonymity, replacing it with a brash rendering of her own theatrically created persona that was distant and cold — perhaps even shy somewhere deep beneath the veneer — yet dominantly loud, obnoxious and brazen. Kathleen did not seem to care what anyone thought of her behavior — a trait which instigated a great amount of gossip among the prominent ladies' sewing and reading circles.

When Kathleen Carter built her enormous house, she again

44

became the talk of Benton Harbor. She said she inherited some family money which in itself would have been acceptable to the conservative citizens of the city. However, her sudden acquisition of funds was accompanied by exceedingly flamboyant and exorbitant spending about which Kathleen bragged loudly and frequently whenever townsfolk, especially distinguished ones, were around to hear. Many people became irritated when the name Kathleen Carter was mentioned in conversation. Still, as far as Grace knew, none of her outrageous behaviors constituted ill feelings hostile enough to inflict Kathleen with the cuts and bruises that were evident now.

"Might she have fallen down the stairs?" Grace asked when they were driving back to the Shepard house in a tufted leather carriage lent to them by Emily Carter.

"Possibly, but even a fall down the stairs would not produce as many cuts and bruises as Mrs. Kathleen Carter sustained, especially of the type exhibited on both of her hands. She may have been pushed down the stairs, but she was trying to protect herself. Somebody was definitely punching her — she is lucky that none of her ribs were broken — and there are a series of small bruises on her throat that look as if someone was choking her.

"Unfortunately that scoundrel is someone Mrs. Carter is either scared to death of or is protecting for some other reason. Ascertaining the identity of her attacker is far from likely unless she tells us. And one other thing is also certain, she admitted whoever it was into the house. I noticed there was no evidence of forced entry at either door."

"Where was her housemaid?" Grace asked, thinking aloud.

"Good question. The word in town is that Mrs. Carter cannot keep help. You may have observed that she is a most difficult person."

"I see." Grace said.

45

❦ Chapter Seven

A MATTER OF TIME

December passed into January with hopes and blessings for the new year ahead. It was 1896 and the year held economic as well as inventive promise.

A winter storm kept everyone house-bound for several days in late January. Tied together with a rope line, Dan and young Danny made frequent trips to the barn to feed the horses and to break the ice that continually formed on the water trough. Grace could hear the wind battering the sides of the house as she kept the younger children occupied with board games, books and the precious stereopticon they had received for Christmas.

Grace was teaching Susan how to embroider when Helen walked into the parlor and stood for a moment near the wide windows in the center of the room. Snow blew in a direction away from the mottled glass then shifted and pelted the house with a dense white gust. Helen moved a small settee to a vantage point in front of the window and watched. The wind swirled sheets of snow away from the house and she briefly saw the barn before it disappeared again in a violent rush of falling snow.

"It was about this time last year when the *Chicora* went down," she said to no one in particular. "Think how dreadful that must have been for those poor passengers, out on Lake Michigan in a steam ship during a storm like this. The wind blowing the boat in all directions and finally breaking it apart and sinking it."

"It was a ship, Grandma, not a boat," Danny said.

"Whatever is the difference?"

"A boat can be carried on board a ship, but a ship is too large to be carried on anything."

"Well, it was not big enough to stay afloat in any case."

Helen shuddered at the thought of an icy death in Lake Michigan and began shuffling restlessly through stacks of calling cards and photographs on the tea table near the windows. She selected a few to look at and sat back in the settee.

Dan glanced up from his copy of *The Evening Press*. "There was an article about the *Chicora* in the paper last week, Mother," Dan said. "It was exactly last year, January of 1895, when that ship was lost. The *Press* said no survivors from the wreck were ever found."

"Gives me the shivers," Susan said, dropping the stitch she was struggling with.

"Keep your eyes on your work, honey," Grace said. "Would you like me to fix it for you?"

Susan handed the small embroidery piece to her mother.

"What were they carrying?" asked Danny. "Chicago townsfolk would not have been traveling to these parts in winter."

"They sailed to Milwaukee and were on their way back with a load of flour when they encountered a blizzard in a January storm similar to today. When the weather cleared, searchers found wreckage strewn from here to South Haven," Dan said.

"But no survivors?" Susan asked, proudly using the word she had just learned from her father.

Grace wished that Susan had not been within earshot of this conversation, but she said nothing and concentrated on the needlework, stitching smoothly and tying off the loose ends Susan had left hanging from the back of the cloth.

"I am afraid not, honey." Dan said. He observed his wife and young daughter thoughtfully. He could see the top of Grace's head — a coil of dark brown hair wound softly at the crown — bent over Susan's handiwork as she removed the mistake Susan had made and continued working for a few stitches more.

"Grace," Dan said. "Bowersox has an article here about a terrible commotion on Territorial, near the *Evening News* plant, where two drunken men were chasing each other and one of the fellows was stabbed."

"As the editor of the *Press*, might he be attempting to stain the competition by association with such a story?" Grace said with an insight into media competition that surprised her even as she spoke.

"A cynic! Grace, that is so unlike you. Although I suppose he could have used Frick's Shoe Store as a reference place to the scuffle. In any case, my point is," Dan said, raising his eyebrows. He appreciated his wife's intelligence, yet her recent independence made him somewhat uneasy. "You have been taking quite an interest in that Carter woman — "

"And her child, Dan," Grace interjected.

"Yes, well, I simply wish to caution you. Driving through that part of town might not be altogether safe."

"I promise I will take care, although . . ." Grace hesitated and then decided against finishing her statement. She had been about to say that no one is truly safe, our lives are all simply a matter of time.

Since Karla's influence had entered into Grace's psyche, Grace had become more outspoken and bolder than she had ever been. Very often now, words came out of Grace's mouth that she knew were from Karla's world. And as much as Grace held hope for the future, it had become increasingly evident through Karla's wisdom that people were destined to repeat the mistakes of the past over and over again.

She made a silent vow to learn from the new opportunities Karla Cifelli had brought into her life. She would not allow herself to become one of the masses of people who shut the doors on new thoughts and ideas. Grace vowed to remain open to the challenges before her and to attempt to solve them with intelligence and kindness.

❦ Chapter Eight

A SCUFFLE AT THE YORE OPERA HOUSE

Grace had delivered meals to Kathleen and Emily Carter on the day after Christmas and then again a week later. She had not seen them since, but the mysterious circumstances of Kathleen's horrific beating had been constantly on her mind.

When the wind finally quieted after the storm, Grace hitched Belle to the sleigh and ventured into town. The sun was shining brightly on drifts of new snow. Happy to be outside, Belle kicked up her heels and threw wispy clouds of breath into the crystal cold air.

Grace drove west down the hill on Territorial Road. When she neared Sixth Street, the Yore Opera House's imposing four- story structure came into view. Its height overshadowed the lower wooden buildings around it and the detailed brickwork and ornate cornices lent the structure an aristocratic air.

Although most of the Yore Block was engaged by the opera house, three small businesses occupied its lower story. Grace looked for a place to secure Belle and the carriage near Bernstein's Clothing Stock where she thought she might browse a bit, and maybe wander into the back of the building where Austin's Bakery was located. The aroma of cinnamon buns drifted onto the street and Grace impulsively developed a taste for something sweet at the scent.

As she knotted Belle's reins to a vacant hitching post, Grace noticed Kathleen Carter's horse and carriage tied up near the opera house's side door. Abandoning her plans to shop, Grace headed up the narrow flight of stairs to the door.

She knocked loudly on the heavy wooden door and was about to walk around to the front, when Kathleen Carter opened

49

the door just a crack and peered out.

"Yes?" Kathleen said coldly. She was wearing a low-cut dress which exposed her neck and shoulders along with a daring expanse of her breasts. Grace was relieved to see that the swelling and bruises had disappeared; however, she wished Kathleen would take heed of the talk around town. It would make life so much easier for her and for Emily if she would attempt to conform even a little bit to the dictates of modern society. This brazen show of cleavage in the daytime would surely start the gossiping tongues wagging again.

"Hello, Mrs. Carter," Grace said ignoring the almost closed door and Kathleen's distant manner. "I was shopping and noticed your carriage. You are looking very well. How would you be feeling today?"

"Much better, thank you very much, Mrs. Shepard," Kathleen said. A loud crash behind her made her step back and turn around. The door opened wider and Grace stepped to the inside of the back stage of the opera house. It was lit by streams of winter sunlight from the narrow windows and cluttered with disheveled stacks of lumber and tools.

"Whatever is going on?" Grace asked.

"We are, um, rehearsing for a new show. Some scenery must have fallen," Kathleen lied. Even through her thick make-up, Grace could see the color drain away from her face. The sounds of shouting voices came through the thin wall and they did not sound at all like lines being rehearsed. Kathleen tried to force Grace out the door saying, "Play productions do not always run smoothly. Well, thank you again, Mrs. Shepard, I do appreciate your asking — "

Kathleen was interrupted when a stage door banged open and a man came flying through it backwards. He landed and sprang to his feet so fast, Grace was unable to identify who he was. She rushed through the open door in time to see Mr. Will McClanahan, the superintendent of public instruction, crash through a flimsy piece of wooden scenery. He jumped up and over the fallen backdrop and grabbed the first man by the throat, pulled back and slammed his powerful fist into the first man's bloodied jaw. When the man staggered backward, Grace recog-

50

nized him as Mr. Evan Howell, one of Benton Harbor's leading iron manufacturers.

Grace was appalled to witness these two men fighting. Both of them were prominent citizens of Benton Harbor. They were not the sort of gentlemen that one would expect to find handling their differences like common ruffians. She remembered Dan's admonishment of the evening before. She hoped he would not learn of her presence here. As far as Grace knew, there was no apparent reason for either man to be in the opera house and she suddenly felt a pang of guilt for being here as well, but curiosity overtook her and she stood steadfastly inside the theater.

"What is this about, Mrs. Carter?" Grace demanded.

"Mrs. Shepard, I am sorry but this is none of your business. It is a difference of opinion, nothing more." Kathleen turned away leaving the scent of strong perfume in her wake. Grace had the distinct feeling that Kathleen knew exactly what it was about and that it had something to do with her so-called accident on the stairwell of her home. Whatever it was, Kathleen was not inclined to reveal its purpose to Grace at this juncture.

The front door of the opera house opened sending a wide beam of sunlight down the darkened center aisle. Silhouettes of three men crossed the threshold.

"Hey! You hoodlums are wrecking my set," one of the men shouted. He broke into a run taking the stairs from the floor of the auditorium to the stage in two strides and grabbing Will McClanahan who was staggering toward the fallen Howell with a murderous look in his eyes.

McClanahan was stocky and strong. He threw off the stage manager and continued toward Howell who was lying on the floor. Howell's nose and lip were bleeding profusely and he was clutching his stomach with both hands.

It took two of the stage hands to hold off McClanahan. Wild physical rage had taken over his sensibilities. After several minutes he regained control, but before he did he shot a terrifying glance at Kathleen. In that split second, Grace felt the fear spread out around Kathleen. Something here was very wrong, Grace thought, and she resolved to find out what it was.

Evan Howell was on his feet and heading out the door.

51

"What about my set?" the stage manager shouted. "Who is going to compensate for the damages?"

"Ask him," Howell said pointing at McClanahan. "He is the one with the uncontrollable temper."

McClanahan started toward him, but one of the stage hands intervened. McClanahan had calmed himself enough not to pursue Howell. He shook off the stage hand and swore under his breath. Grace could not hear what he said then and a moment later the leading citizen demeanor was back in control. He slapped at the dust on his trousers and jacket.

"This is *my* opera house now," McClanahan said to the stage manager. "Make a list of the damages and leave it with corresponding amounts in the box office. You will be compensated along with the remainder of your expenses. You and your crew are finished. Now, if you will excuse me." He marched out the front door without looking back.

"Mr. McClanahan is the proprietor of the opera house now?" Grace asked incredulously. "What about Mr. J.A. Simon and Miss Lily Cross?"

"This is news to me," Kathleen lied again. Even her lavish creams, emollients and rouge could not hide the guilty look on her face.

"But you are here. Would you not work for him now?"

"I suppose so, if what he says is true."

"Mrs. Carter," Grace said. "Mr. McClanahan is a powerful man, but that does not give him the right to intimidate you or to threaten you with bodily harm."

"He is not threatening me," Kathleen said unconvincingly. She cut her eyes toward Evan Howell with an expression Grace could not interpret. The actress' mask she normally flaunted had slipped away, replaced by fear and confusion.

Grace was suddenly certain that it was Will McClanahan who had badly beaten her. She tried again to reason with Kathleen. "Mrs. Carter, your fear a moment ago was — "

"Your perceptions do not interest me, Mrs. Shepard," Kathleen snapped. The theatrical mask was back in place. "As I said before, this incident is clearly none of your business. I am fully capable of handling my own affairs. Good day, Mrs.

Shepard. Mr. Howell." Kathleen pivoted sharply and exited through the back stage door, slamming it behind her and leaving a drift of sawdust in her wake.

Grace helped Evan Howell to his feet and offered to give him a ride home.

"No thank you, Mrs. Shepard," Howell said. He was blotting his face with a blood-soaked handkerchief. "My own rig is just outside."

Kathleen was no where in sight as they walked through the ruined scenery to the side door. Howell said something about returning to his foundry and they parted at the bottom of the narrow staircase on the street. Grace untied Belle's reins and climbed into the carriage. She tossed a fur throw over her knees and lightly flicked the reins. She turned the horse west onto Main Street and Belle's hooves clattered over the brick pavement.

Theodora was busy with a patient when Grace arrived at her office. Grace sat down outside of the examining room and waited for her friend. The sparse waiting room contained a glassed-in cabinet of medical books and two chairs with a low table between them. Grace picked up a copy of a magazine entitled *Headlight Flashes* and leafed through the dog-earred pages.

She had just settled on an article about the Eastman Springs health resort, when the door to the examining room opened and Theodora ushered Mrs. Hilda McClanahan through the foyer to the front door. Mrs. McClanahan dropped one of Theodora's medicine vials into her handbag and slouched out the door with her head hanging forward and her eyes on the floor. She was wearing a woolen navy dress with an over-sized linen collar that drooped over her rounded shoulders and gave her the appearance of a turtle sticking its neck out.

"That poor woman . . ." Theodora said when Mrs. McClanahan was gone, "her husband is a bully with a nasty temper. I suspect he beats her at home, but she steadfastly denies it. I suppose that she has no where else to go, but I wish that I could convince her to get herself and her children safely away from him, even for a while. Maybe that would shake some sense into him."

"Your conclusion fits with today's exhibition of Mr.

McClanahan's behavior." Grace said. She related the incident with Will McClanahan, Evan Howell and Kathleen Carter at the opera house.

"So you think he is the one responsible for Mrs. Carter's injuries?" Theodora said. She thought a moment, then added, "Mrs. McClanahan has made appointments here many times to request pain medication for headaches, cuts and bruises. She always has implausible excuses as to how she incurred the injuries."

"Just like Mrs. Kathleen Carter."

"That is so. You know, Grace, now that I think about it, they have something else in common — although, I am not sure it bears any significance — the McClanahans came here from Detroit about two years before Mrs. Carter arrived in Benton Harbor with her daughter. The Carters also moved here from Detroit."

"Did Mrs. McClanahan tell you that?" Grace asked eagerly. Her intuition suggested that the apparent coincidence was very significant. Grace had been acutely aware of Karla's inner voice that had grown increasingly vocal since the holidays had passed into the new year. The voice was definitely speaking to her now, with an authority and an insight that Grace could not deny.

"She must have. I am certain it is written in their medical records," Theodora answered.

"This is a connection we need to explore further. And I would like to learn what Mr. McClanahan and Mr. Howell were fighting about and why they were in the opera house in the first place."

"You said Mr. Howell walked away with injuries?"

"His handkerchief was soaked with blood," Grace said. "I feel certain that Mr. McClanahan initiated the scuffle. We know he has a violent temper. Mr. Howell mentioned it, too."

"This may be an opportune time for me to pay a visit to Mr. Evan Howell's foundry before he has a chance to think too long about what happened today. Mrs. McClanahan was the last patient scheduled for this afternoon. Would you have the time to accompany me?"

"Of course. The children are all in school and Helen is preparing our supper." Grace replied. She had already started for her coat and hat.

Theodora closed her office and they rode smoothly over the icy pavement to the Howell Iron Manufacturers. Belle trotted along at a brisk pace while Grace guided her with only a gentle touch on the reins.

The women decided that Theodora might be able to get Evan Howell talking if she approached him alone. She had a curious way of listening that made people want to talk — often more than they had planned — and Evan Howell was likely to be more forthcoming about the causes of his injuries to a doctor.

Grace dropped Theodora off at the front door of the Howell Manufacturing Plant. They arranged to meet again at D. Hunt's grocery store which was only a short distance from the foundry. Grace turned Belle back toward Main Street and consulted her list for the things she needed: white sugar, graham flour and hard candy. Mr. Hunt's grocery purported to have everything for the modern kitchen and if a desired item was not in stock, he would gladly order it.

The wooden floorboards creaked when Grace walked inside the store. She loved the smells of the spices and coffee beans that Mr. Hunt kept in big glass jars on the shelves.

"Mornin' Miz Shepard," Mr. Hunt said, looking up from his newspaper. He was standing behind the counter near the cash register wearing a familiar green apron looped over his head and tied securely around his waist.

"Good morning Mr. Hunt, how is business today?"

"Lots of folks gettin' out after the snow."

"Myself included," Grace said handing him her list.

"'Course, I could always use a few more gracious customers like yourself, Miz Shepard."

"Thank you, Mr. Hunt. I will mention that to my neighbors."

"I'd be much obliged to you."

"Not at all. I am happy to do it. By the way, I heard that Mr. Will McClanahan bought the opera house from Mr. J.A. Simon and Miss Lily Cross."

"Heard that too. The new show's s'posed to be a humdinger. 'Course they always say that." He scooped the flour and sugar one by one from the neatly organized jars and placed Grace's order on the countertop.

"I was unaware that the opera house was for sale," Grace prodded.

"From what I gather — but you didn't hear it from me — the place was in bad financial shape. Never has been profitable, not since Pat Yore built the place. McClanahan bought it for the back taxes. Miss Lily Cross is — " He made a twirling motion with his index finger next to his temple. "She, well, you know how bad things got after her folks passed away. Anyway, she failed to keep things up and that nephew of hers Simon wasn't much better. McClanahan sort of bailed her out from what I heard. You know the two are next door neighbors."

"Yes, I know."

The bell jangled over the entrance and Theodora hurried inside letting the wooden door slam behind her.

Mr. Hunt wrapped the groceries into brown paper and tied the bundle with twine.

"Mum's the word, now," he whispered handing the bundle to Grace and greeting Theodora with a broad smile. "What can I do for you today, Dr. Goodhart?"

"Nothing today, thank you. Unless you have some of that good anise candy left from Christmas?"

"Not a drop. Got some fine lemon candies here, though."

"One cannot go wrong with lemon, Mr. Hunt. I do believe I will have a few. Just a small amount, mind you."

"Well?" Grace said as soon as they were outside again.

"Mr. Howell was his usual talkative self. That man is in need of companionship. I fixed a compress for his headache and gave him some Laudenum to ease the pain. I did not have to coax him a bit about the origin of his bruises. He lambasted Mr. Will McClanahan from here to next week. Apparently, Mr. Howell was paying our Mrs. Kathleen Carter a friendly visit when Mr. McClanahan barged in and ordered him to leave. Mr. Howell would not budge and when Mr. McClanahan grabbed him by the lapels, Evan Howell pushed him off and you know what happened next."

"Mr. McClanahan is getting very proprietary about people he perceives as his property." Grace said.

56

"You mean Mrs. Carter?"

"And his wife."

"Now that Mr. McClanahan is the proprietor of the opera house, I imagine he views everyone there as his subordinate."

"When did he come into ownership?"

"I do not know exactly."

"I was not aware that the superintendent's salary was quite so rich."

"According to Mr. Hunt, Miss Lily and Mr. Simon were in bad financial straits and Mr. McClanahan bought the theater for the back taxes."

"I do not see how that can be. I attend nearly every show and the house is always full. The shows are frequently held over for additional performances."

"Mr. Hunt said that the opera house has never turned a profit. He also indicated that Miss Lily has gone a little crazy." Grace twirled her finger imitating Mr. Hunt's gesture.

"Well, she always has been eccentric, but . . ." Theodora watched as her words drifted on moist puffs of breath which disappeared in the cold winter air. She pondered the matter and continued, "It appears we had better look in on Miss Lily Cross."

"Now?"

"I cannot today. I have plans for this evening."

"Soon, then."

"Yes, as soon as possible."

When they reached Theodora's office, Grace drove around to the back where Theodora resided. The house, a combination of office space and living quarters, was a neat white frame structure in the center of town. Theodora maintained a waiting room and an examining room in the front. Her large bedroom and kitchen located at the back of the house had adjacent wood-burning stoves which shared a chimney. Theodora kept both rooms heated with wood that some of her less affluent patients provided in exchange for medical services.

Grace came in to get warm before driving home. "Would it be unethical for me to look at your files on the McClanahans and the Carters?" Grace asked.

"Well, yes . . . I believe so, Grace. But perhaps I might read some of the salient information aloud and you might overhear a small bit of it." Theodora said, winking at Grace. "Would you be so kind as to prepare a pot of tea while I retrieve the records?"

According to Theodora's files, Will and Hilda McClanahan had three children. The family had moved to Benton Harbor from Detroit fifteen years ago when he was hired as the superintendent of public instruction for the Benton Harbor schools.

Hilda McClanahan suffered from a variety of ailments ranging from aches in the head, sleeplessness and female disorders, to stomach aches, despondency and back pains. Notes in the file suggested that she was forgetful and often absentminded. There were several incidents when she misplaced her medications and Theodora had refilled them. There were no notes in the file regarding Mr. McClanahan.

"He has never been in," Theodora said accepting the steaming cup of tea that Grace handed to her.

Theodora opened the Carter file and began scanning the information she had recorded over the years. There was nothing outstanding in the file about Mrs. Carter or Emily. Emily had weathered the usual childhood diseases in the thirteen years she had lived here. Prior to that, the first two years of her life in Detroit had been unremarkable. She was a healthy, sturdy child.

"Theodora," Grace said almost to herself when Theodora finished with the medical file. "Did you ever notice the resemblance between Emily Carter and Mr. Will McClanahan?"

Theodora was about to take a sip of tea and stopped short, she held her cup in front of her and stared over it at Grace. "The forest through the trees, Grace . . . you are absolutely right. The child does favor the McClanahans. If Mrs. Kathleen Carter and Mr. Will McClanahan are still seeing each other that explains his irrational behavior at the opera house."

"It could also explain how he knew Miss Lily Cross was in arrears financially," Grace said.

"How is that?"

"I am conjecturing now, but do you remember when Miss Lily let the Carters reside at her house in exchange for housekeeping help when they first arrived in town? Miss Lily took a fancy to Kathleen and was, I believe, instrumental in getting her a job in the opera house when it was constructed eleven years ago. The two have been friends of a sort ever since. Kathleen, you will recall, did not have a penny to her name when she came here and now look at her, that house she built is worth a fortune, not to mention the furnishings. Who knows how much Miss Lily confided to Kathleen?"

"This entire train of thought makes me wonder if Mr. McClanahan has been taking advantage of her or if she has been conspiring with him all along." Theodora said.

A loud knocking on the front door brought their speculation to an abrupt halt.

Theodora returned to the kitchen a moment later to inform Grace that her evening caller had arrived early. Grace swallowed the last of her tea and quietly let herself out the back door.

She passed the McClanahan house and was about to pass Miss Lily Cross' house when she turned Belle into Miss Lily's long driveway. I absolutely cannot stay long, Grace thought, I promised Helen I would help with supper.

Resolving to make a quick visit, Grace guided Belle toward Miss Lily's hitching post.

❦ Chapter Nine

MISS LILY CROSS

The front door was ajar despite the cold weather. As Grace stepped across the wide wooden porch, she could hear Miss Lily singing loudly and playing her piano inside. Her voice was a breathy soprano that carried well over the din of the out-of-tune piano.

Lily Cross lived alone in a house that sprawled from one side street to another along Main Street. Her father had been one of Benton Harbor's first settlers, traveling to the midwest from New York state in the early 1800s. Her only sibling, a sister, had married young and produced one child, J.A. Simon, who currently served as the manager of the opera house.

As the younger of the two sisters, Miss Lily had grown up in an overly protective environment and was encouraged to live at home well into adulthood. When her mother died, Lily felt obligated to remain with her father. By the time the family home passed into Lily's hands, she had become an aging spinster with little knowledge of the world around her.

"Miss Lily?" Grace called out from the foyer.

"Come in, come in," Lily Cross called back in a sing-song voice. She was singing a repetitious lyric that Grace did not recognize.

"Miss Lily, I wonder if we could talk for a moment about the opera house — "

"It is gone," Lily sang out. She worked the words into the senseless lyric and kept repeating, "it is gone, it is gone, it is gone." She leaned precariously away from the piano and closed her eyes. The stretch of her bony arms to the keyboard seemed to be the only thing preventing her from falling backward off of the piano stool.

"I know it is gone," Grace said gently. "I want to know why you sold it."

"They said I had no money." Miss Lily said throwing her hands in the air and banging them down again on the keyboard.

"Who said?"

"Everybody." Lily said flatly. She stopped playing and stood up with exaggerated elegance. Rouge was smeared haphazardly across her cheekbones and red lipstick surrounded her mouth overscoring her lips by some distance in several places.

"Some sherry, my dear?"

"Thank you. Miss Lily, did Mr. Will McClanahan say you had no money?"

"Oh yes. Here is your sherry, dear." Lily handed Grace a tiny cut-glass goblet of rosy liquid.

"How did Mr. McClanahan know about your finances?"

"He has kept my books for years, ever since father died. I really could not be bothered. I have my stage career, you know." She downed her sherry with a flourish and poured another.

"Then it was Mr. McClanahan who failed to pay your taxes?"

"That is due to our extreme lack of money! Are you not listening to me?" Lily plopped back onto the piano stool and began pounding on the keys. She ceased as suddenly as she had begun and rose again from the stool. "I feel a chill in the air, are you cold, my dear?" Lily asked.

Grace nodded. Now that she knew that Mr. McClanahan was in charge of the bookkeeping, she wondered what he had been doing with the opera house's income all these years. The performances she and Dan attended had always been full. Theodora had said the same thing. Grace had assumed that the theater was a profitable venture. But she knew that the management was not spending box office proceeds on staff salaries. Pianist Fred Null had mentioned to Grace that he received a mere three dollars for a night's work. He had been after young Simon for a pay raise for months.

The only building improvement in recent memory was the addition of electric lighting. The beautiful structure was in a state of slowly decaying elegance. The auditorium seats were becoming shabby and the interior paint was peeling — much like Miss Lily herself, Grace mused.

Lily strode purposefully out of the room and returned carrying an intricately carved dining room chair. She banged it against the floor and Grace jumped back as large pieces of splintered wood scattered across the floor. Lily gathered up the pieces and tossed them one by one onto a bed of embers in the grate.

Grace watched as Lily removed a novel from the book shelf and carelessly placed it on top of the chair legs already smouldering in the fire. Glancing around the barren room, Grace realized that Miss Lily must have been burning her belongings for a long time. When was the last time she had seen Lily Cross? Grace had not known the Cross family well, but she felt guilty at the sight of Miss Lily's degenerating appearance and her odd behavior.

"Miss Lily, I am on my way home for supper, would you like to come and stay the night?" Grace suggested gently.

Lily gazed up from the fireplace with bright eyes and brushed her sooty hands on the folds of her skirt. The aura around her body was a muddy mix of colors that swirled randomly above her head as she grabbed another volume from the bookcase and opened it as if to read aloud. She held it high in her hands and Grace noticed that the book was upsidedown. Lily ran an index finger down one page, then snapped the book closed. She looked wildly up at Grace.

"A dinner invitation at this late hour? Obviously I have made other plans. Mr. McClanahan will undoubtably deliver a meal soon. Perhaps another occasion, dear." Lily threw the book onto the fire and stalked back to the piano dismissing Grace as she crossed the floor in front of her.

Grace closed the heavy front door securely and stepped carefully across the snow covered porch. Belle stood patiently by the hitching post. Grace untied the leather reins and hugged the big horse's neck. She needed a steady feeling just then and Belle felt warm and solid. Some things could be counted upon in this life and some things could not. Miss Lily Cross, Grace decided, had encountered one too many unsteady things.

CHAPTER TEN

HIDE IN PLAIN SIGHT

By the next morning, a cover of fresh snow had fallen. From her bedroom window, Grace could see Dan's footprints leading to the barn, then the tracks of the hay wagon disappearing into the orchards.

Dan was one of life's steady people. Grace gave a silent prayer for him and thought of Miss Lily. She amended her prayer to include assistance for Miss Lily and hurried down the narrow staircase.

Young Danny was helping Susan with her coat and hat when Grace entered the kitchen. No longer in school himself, Danny drove the younger children to and from school every day. Grace kissed them all good-by and began drying the breakfast dishes that Helen had stacked in the wire drainer.

"I must go into town again today," Grace said. "Is there anything I can get for you?"

Helen looked up from her mending. "You went to town just yesterday," Helen said with a touch of irritation in her tone. "I thought we were going to wash and iron the slipcovers for the parlor. It is high time we readied that room for spring. I simply cannot accomplish such heavy work alone, Grace."

"I am truly sorry Helen, but this is important." Grace said stacking the finished plates on an open shelf in the pantry. She folded the damp linen dish towel in half and placed it on the rack to dry. Grace self-consciously smoothed a long strand of her brown hair and avoided Helen's eyes as she left the kitchen.

"Do what you have to do," Helen said after her, "I will attend to the household chores." She did not sigh and for that, Grace was grateful.

Grace knew that Helen expected more of her. When she had moved into the big house with Dan, Helen had been delighted at the prospect of companionship with her daughter-in-law. But self reserve was so firmly ingrained in Grace's nature, that she found

63

it impossible to form an emotional bond with Helen. Helen's demands reminded Grace too much of her own mother. Grace had tried and been unable to fill the void within her mother since Grace's baby sister had died. She was now unable to take such a risk again. For Helen's sake, Grace wished she was more of the daughter-in-law that Helen wanted.

Her boots crunched on the snow as Grace walked to the barn wondering what her life might have been like if that baby girl had not died. Would her mother have loved her more as a person in her own right? Would she have more to give to Helen now? Would her life have been more complete with a sister? Happier? More carefree?

Grace surveyed the pastoral scene around the barn. A clear blue sky hung overhead. The air was brisk and clean. Fresh snow covered every imperfection giving the orchards a look of peaceful renewal.

This was the life she had been given, Grace decided. She could not change what had already happened. She could not bring her baby sister back to life and she could not make her mother love her more. Her mother had done the best she could in raising her, Grace felt certain of that. There was no point in dwelling on the problems of the past, they were gone forever.

Grace knew she had today and she intended to make the most of it. There were people in this world that she could help. She climbed into the carriage and resolved to look ahead and to act with optimism.

Grace arrived at Theodora's house a little before nine o'clock hoping that her friend would still be inside. It was Theodora's usual day off and she tended to get an early start on her chores and errands. Grace found Theodora in the kitchen washing her long blond hair over a tub of hot water.

"Once a week whether it needs it or not," Theodora joked. "I have been trying to convince some of my patients that their hair will not rot away with regular washings. Some of them still think that too much washing will infect them with a mysterious and deadly disease."

She squeezed water from her hair with both hands. Then, she coiled her waist length hair into a towel and sat down with Grace.

"Help yourself to some tea, I think there is half a pot left."

Grace told her about Miss Lily's dementia and her suspicions of Will McClanahan's misuse of opera house funds. "The problem is," Grace said, "if Mr. Will McClanahan has been doing Miss Lily's bookwork for years, it is likely he has his covert activities completely covered up and all of the legal documents properly filed. There is also the possibility that I am wrong about the funds, but I fail to see how the opera house could possibly be losing as much money as he purports."

Theodora moved to the fireplace and blotted her hair with the towel. She started combing the ends, working her way up through the tangled, long strands. "I have not seen Miss Lily since her mother — rest her soul — died. And that was when? Three years ago? About the time all this business started with Mr. McClanahan. I remember then that Miss Lily did not leave the house even to go to the cemetery, which I thought was extremely odd at the time, but I assumed it was due to her overcoming grief.

"Now, if she is having her groceries delivered . . . and if Mr. McClanahan handles all of her personal matters along with the money management at the opera house . . . and she is not even venturing out of doors for firewood . . . does she ever take leave of the house? Miss Lily has always been a weak person, her parents let her remain a baby too long; but it does sound almost as though she has tipped into madness.

"Even though she has apparently made it easy for Mr. McClanahan to take advantage of her, I cannot imagine how he could have accomplished all of this treachery alone. He had to have help to juggle the books at the opera house. Who else besides J.A. Simon works at the box office, do you know, Grace?"

"Miss Emily Carter. She has ever since she was twelve years old. She is a very mature girl."

"Miss Emily is fifteen now, so her employment has extended to three years. Grace, there are one too many coincidences which originated three years ago." Theodora had finished combing her hair and was separating it for braids.

"Miss Emily quit school when she went to work. It is likely that Mr. McClanahan taught her everything about the systems of box office accounting. She would never have the wherewithal to know the difference between honest and crooked methods."

65

Grace said. "That poor child, if Mr. McClanahan is her father maybe in some twisted way, he thinks he has been helping her."

"There is little doubt in my mind that Mr. Will McClanahan knows exactly what he is doing. What we need is proof of his actions for the sheriff. What do you say to strolling over to the opera house. The cast is in rehearsals, maybe there will be enough confusion for one of us to slip inside the office and peruse the records."

"Mercy me, Theodora. Are you suggesting that we break into the office?"

"Certainly not! I am merely suggesting that we wander over there, and on the off chance that the office is open, we simply take a look inside." Theodora said. "If we do not, who will?"

"Sheriff Knapp?"

"On what basis? That we think Mr. Will McClanahan has literally stolen the opera house from Miss Lily? That he has taken advantage of her dementia for his own personal gain? I am certain that any paperwork filed by the superintendent of public instruction regarding property transfers would have been handled properly. Unless we uncover actual evidence, he is free to continue with his underhanded ways. Consider what he has already done to Kathleen Carter and to his own wife and family. That man is a menace. He needs to be prevented from further immoral actions."

"What are we looking for?" Grace asked, rising from the kitchen table and putting on her coat. She secured its fur collar with a hook and balanced a matching fur hat on the top of her head. She looked inquiringly at Theodora for an answer to her question.

"I have no idea, Grace. We will see when we get there."

"Hopefully, something that we can take directly to the sheriff."

"Removing anything would be stealing, you know."

"Well, then something that we can tell the sheriff about."

The door to the ticket office was locked from the lobby. Grace had tried the glass knob as soon as they walked through the front door. They could hear noises coming from the auditorium, but no one was present in the theater's entryway.

66

"They are probably on stage and in the backstage area, too," Grace said softly. "I know where there is another entrance to the office through the back hall, but we have to go through the auditorium and around behind the stage to get to it. People will see us."

"You are a respected theater patron, are you not?" Theodora said flatly. "We will simply walk right through the house as if we have important business here. It is the old *hide in plain sight* theory."

"And what is the old *hide in plain sight theory*, pray tell?"

"Act like you know what you are doing and people will believe that you know what you are doing. It is quite simple. You and I, Grace, are a couple of upstanding citizens interested in the inner workings of the theater. Smile at anyone who looks in your direction."

Grace nodded to Theodora that she was ready to follow her through the auditorium and into the office area.

Theodora adjusted her tam dislodging a long blonde tendril in the process. Her face spread into a tight smile that immediately diminished into concern for her friend. "What is the very worst consequence that might befall us here?" she whispered to Grace. "That Mr. Will McClanahan might discover us? We simply will be too quick for the scoundrel. We will beat him at his own game!"

She grasped Grace's arm and they staunchly promenaded toward the auditorium door.

There were a couple of men sitting in the center section midway to the stage. Grace recognized one of them as Mr. J.A. Simon. She waved to him and he waved back. Bright lights shone from the balcony throwing the rest of the vast auditorium into shadowy darkness. Theodora, with Grace close behind her, strode down the left aisle toward the back stage door. Set crews were working and actors sat in corners studying scripts, but no one said a word to the two women or even gave them more than a passing glance.

"See?" Theodora's expression seemed to say. "It is no problem at all if you act like you know exactly where you are going." She kept moving at a brisk pace toward what presumably was a back door to the office and dressing room section of the rambling building.

The first door Theodora tried opened easily, revealing a long and narrow corridor lined with doors to dressing rooms and storage areas. Some of the doors were ajar; murmurs of people working inside could be vaguely heard from the hallway.

Puzzled, Theodora looked back at Grace.

"It is this way," Grace whispered, "at the end of the hallway."

Grace knocked on the closed door to the office and waited. When there was no answer, she tried the faceted glass knob and it turned in her hand. Looking over her shoulder, Grace entered the dingy office and held the door open for Theodora to enter. She left it open just a crack and stood silently listening for breath or movement in the hallway behind them. There was nothing.

The office was cluttered except for the stand-up desk at the box office window. Blank diagrams of the auditorium seats were stacked in a pile in the center of the desk. Theodora quickly started going through drawers. Grace pulled open the top drawer of an oak filing cabinet and fingered through the files. She located one labeled "Murphy's World" and opened it. It was the last show she and Dan had attended.

"Theodora, look at this," she whispered. "These diagrams show half or less of the seats filled for these shows. This is the night that Dan and I attended and it was a full house."

"Are you sure?" Theodora studied the seating chart. It indicated that three-fourths of the house seats were empty.

"Yes, I am absolutely certain. It was Dan's birthday."

Grace flipped through the rest of the file. "This show was held over for two extra weekends. There are no seating charts here for the hold-over shows."

"So Mr. Will McClanahan simply is not recording all of his receipts. He has sell-out performances, but only indicates partial attendance. It would be easy to accomplish this deception since most of the ticket sales are small amounts of cash."

Grace frowned and ran her finger along the top of one of the charts. She said, "This is untrained childish script. I have not seen Mr. McClanahan's penmanship, but my educated guess is that this is Miss Emily Carter's handwriting. She is the one who attends to the box office most nights."

"I think we need to pay young Miss Carter a visit," Theodora said sliding a file drawer closed.

She scrutinized the room. It appeared exactly as they had found it.

Grace edged toward the door and peered through the opening. The corridor was clear. They slipped through the office door, closing it quietly behind them, and hurried to the exit.

❦ Chapter Eleven

Miss Emily Carter

More than two months passed before Grace and Theodora were able to get together to pay a visit to young Emily Carter. An outbreak of measles that spread from St. Joseph to Benton Harbor prevented Theodora from leaving her office except to make house calls on advanced cases of the disease.

Grace and Helen had helped with the severe cases near their farm. Fortunately, Susan had not been afflicted with the disease. She had gradually gained strength since her bout with the fever. Even when one of her sisters came down with the measles, Susan remained immune.

As spring passed into summer, Grace fretted that Mr. Will McClanahan had had ample time to further revise the records in the opera house box office. She worried that they would be unable to discover the evidence needed to prove their suspicions.

Theodora remained hopeful that Miss Emily Carter would be able to shed some light upon the record keeping practices that Mr. Will McClanahan had installed in the opera house since he had taken it over.

"Summer is definitely in the air," Theodora said as she climbed into Grace's carriage. "I feel almost giddy to get out of the office and away from patients covered with spots!"

"Martha's children are well again. Everyone around the farm seems to be back in excellent health," Grace reported. "And I am relieved to say that I am firmly in Helen's good graces. Since I spent so much time inside tending to Louise, we were able to get all of the spring cleaning finished."

They drove through downtown Benton Harbor and turned south toward the Carter mansion. Belle tossed her head in the air as they passed the paddock where Buster was confined. He trotted up to the fence and gazed at them.

Miss Emily Carter was working on an intricate needlepoint

canvas when Theodora knocked on the carved wooden frame of the front door. The center of the door was set with decorative leaded glass. Theodora strained her eyes to see through the wavy pane while Grace secured Belle to the hitching post and hurried up the steps.

When Miss Emily opened the door with her canvas in hand, Grace was struck immediately by the youth and sweetness of this child. She felt a swift pang of guilt for suspecting young Miss Emily of any wrongdoing and fervently hoped they would learn that she was as innocent as she appeared.

"What a pleasant surprise," Emily said politely. She offered tea and they declined perhaps a bit too hastily. Emily glanced at them questioningly for a moment, then shrugged off any doubt. Like most children in 1896, Emily Carter did exactly as she was told. Adults were respected merely for the fact that they were grown. Their actions were viewed by children as being absolutely correct.

"Let us repair to the parlor, then," Emily said. "I would be honored to show you the needlework I have been laboring over, if you have the time, that is."

Emily proudly led them on a tour of the parlor where piles of handworked needlepointed pillows were displayed on the overstuffed furniture. Grace searched for a spot on the settee where she might squeeze in comfortably. Such a place was not to be found. She remained standing as Emily chattered happily about her mother's prized possessions and her own contributions to the furnishings in the room.

Hanging on one wall was a crowded arrangement of needlepoint pictures in ornately gilded frames. The Carters — like many wealthy Victorians — had spent a great deal of time and money on detailed appointments for their home. Every practical item was gaudily adorned with enameled paint, porcelain flowers, tassels and fringe. Many fanciful pieces took their places in the parlor as nothing more useful than fussy objects to look at and to dust. With heavy velvet draperies hanging over thick layers of carpeting upon which masses of elaborate furniture had been placed, the Carter's parlor was a stuffy, overpowering room.

"The cloth I am working on at present is intended as a cover

71

for the piano stool," Emily declared with pleasure. Then, noticing the faces of Grace and Theodora as they feigned interest in her tour, Emily caught herself and apologetically said, "But, you must forgive me, you ladies journeyed here for a purpose, not just to hear a silly girl babble on about her handiwork. Please, Mrs. Shepard, Dr. Goodhart, do sit down."

Grace sat on the edge of a horsehair chair which was already more than half occupied by a bevy of pillows. She felt herself sliding unsteadily on its slippery surface. It would be impossible to sit comfortably on any of the furniture in this busy room. She searched her mind for words to explain their uninvited calling and none came. She shifted uneasily on the edge of the chair and hoped that she would not slide off of it and onto the floor.

Finally, after what seemed to Grace like hours but was in fact only a few moments, Theodora said, "Miss Emily, dear, we need to procure some important information and we hope you are just the person to enlighten us."

Emily brightened at the obvious importance of the request made by the respected doctor. She dropped the needlepoint into her lap and looked over at Theodora and then at Grace with questioning eyes that were even wider and more innocent than before.

Theodora continued speaking in her well-modulated voice, enunciating every word carefully, "We are here today on behalf of Miss Lily Cross — "

Emily interrupted the doctor in a youthful rush of emotion. "Oh, gosh, poor Miss Cross, she's gone completely mad. Do you know she will not go outside her house? Why, Mr. McClanahan has to do everything for her, poor thing. He's such a kindly gentleman, don't you think so?" The untrained language of the young girl spilled out in high contrast to that of the educated doctor.

Theodora leaned forward with an open and unthreatening posture that perfectly balanced the probing nature of the questions she was about to ask. Grace was impressed by the quality Theodora had about her which enticed people to speak the truth in spite of themselves. "You work in the box office at the opera house, is that correct Miss Emily?" Theodora said.

"Yes, Dr. Goodhart."

"Miss Emily, are you aware that Mr. McClanahan has not paid Miss Lily's taxes for several years?" Theodora asked.

"Oh, sure," Emily answered without the slightest hesitation. "That's because the ledgers were in such a mess when we — well, really he — took over. Did you know that Miss Cross would be completely broke and the opera house bankrupt and in complete ruins if it weren't for Mr. McClanahan?"

"Is that so?" Theodora replied in a tone which clearly invited further elaboration.

"Oh, yes," Emily continued nodding her head agreeably. "My mother told me so. She and Mr. McClanahan have both helped Miss Cross on several occasions. You know, being that she's, well, out of her head and all, she can't be trusted, poor thing. Mother sends her clothing and Mrs. McClanahan delivers hot meals to her nearly everyday. Of course, Mr. McClanahan himself is in charge of all of the paperwork, bill paying and such."

"We happened across some opera house files showing only partial receipts for recent performances." Theodora said smiling as disarmingly as if she was complimenting young Emily on her skills with a needle.

Emily looked confused. "I don't understand," she said apologetically.

Theodora explained. "We noticed some — only a few — seating charts which indicated that little more than half of the auditorium was filled during performances we are certain were sold out."

"Of course!" The expression on Emily's face relaxed from confused to capable. Eager to please, she did not seem to question how the doctor happened to have box office information of this nature. "We always use two charts for every performance. Mr. McClanahan says it's important to keep it all separated so we know how our advertising is working; one chart is for the re-served seats and I use a clean chart for tickets sold at the door. All nice and neat, just the way Mr. McClanahan likes it."

"What do you do with the proceeds and the charts from the late sales?" Theodora inquired.

"I leave them for Mr. McClanahan. He comes in after every

73

performance and takes care of the final bookkeeping and the filing." Emily leaned forward in a conspiratorial manner and said, "My employment there is really rather easy, you know. Mr. McClanahan works harder than anyone else and he is always telling me to keep up the good work — he's such a nice man — but I simply don't do that much. Sometimes I help out with the sewing, I'm good at that, and I do some cleaning, but mainly I stand around at the box office. I'm just happy to be there at all with mother rehearsing so much of the time."

"Miss Emily, you have been so very helpful. Thank you ever so much for your time," Theodora said graciously.

Emily's childish face beamed with pleasure.

They chatted for a few more minutes before Grace and Theodora departed. In the carriage, Theodora said, "That rascal has his systems well-ordered. I am sure that Miss Emily has no idea what is going on with his selective bookkeeping but, excuse me, Grace, I would be willing to wager that Mrs. Kathleen Carter is fully aware of the situation and very likely has her hands on the money, too. I also wonder just where Mr. J.A. Simon fits into all of this. I think it is time we let Sheriff Knapp investigate this matter."

"I have been pondering that as well, Theodora. The information we have learned to date is causing me great discomfort. When are you able to free yourself for an appointment at City Hall?"

"Not until next week at the earliest, I am afraid," Theodora replied. "With so many weakened by the measles, it seems that the ague has had an open door to infect them."

"Then, I will call on you as soon as I have heard that the ague has subsided."

❦ Chapter Twelve

SHERIFF KNAPP

It was two weeks before Grace and Theodora were able to make an appointment at the Benton Harbor police headquarters. Once inside the station, they were kept waiting for nearly an hour.

Grace Shepard and Dr. Theodora Goodhart sat on straight-backed wooden chairs, shifting restlessly as the minutes ticked by. Expecting the sheriff to emerge at any moment, both women started in anticipation at the sounds of doors squeaking open and floorboards creaking under heavy footfalls in the old station.

"This is frustrating," Grace whispered to Theodora. "Time is marching on and we are making such slow progress."

Finally, a deputy emerged from an inner office and sauntered toward them down the hallway. He was sloppy and slow moving, with a stomach that swung over the top of his pants like dough rising from a pan. A cigarette drooped from his lips.

Grace and Theodora were sitting on the edge of their chairs, craning their necks in his direction, when he stopped in front of them. A swollen ash fell from his cigarette to the floor; his eyes followed it down and he smudged it into the wooden floor with one booted foot.

"You ladies got some information for Sheriff Knapp?" he said making no attempt to stifle an open yawn that gave Theodora and Grace a full view of the pink roof of his mouth.

"Yes sir, we do. Is the sheriff in?" Theodora asked locking her eyes on the deputy's as she stood up. She stretched to her full height and lifted her chin deliberately. She did not smooth her skirts or fidget with her hair as she stood.

Grace felt a field of tension growing from the circumstances — as yet unknown to the deputy or to the sheriff — of their visit. It was obvious from the deputy's attitude that the women were perceived as an inconvenience in any case, no matter what they

75

had to offer.

"Right this way," he said indifferently, cocking his head in a lazy motion for them to follow his lead to an office off of the main corridor. Grace cast a sideways glance at Theodora who cut her eyes back just long enough for the women to communicate an unspoken message: we are treading in male territory and we have a right to be here; they know it and we know it, but nonetheless, they intend to make this as difficult for us as humanly possible.

Theodora pulled her shoulders back. Her chin jutted out in an expression of firm determination as they rounded the corner into the sheriff's office.

Sheriff Knapp sat at a rolltop desk piled neatly with paperwork. Rows of shelving above the desk were filled with books and more stacks of paper. He rose quickly from his seat and smiled so broadly Grace thought he might drool from the effort. This was his political face, put on for their benefit. As he spoke, his wide expanse of lips shrank back into his face and he shuffled a pile of papers in a gesture that indicated he was a busy man who sincerely hoped that this little appointment would not take up too much of his valuable time.

"Do come in, doctor. Mrs. Shepard," the sheriff said cordially, nodding at each of the women in turn. "Please take a seat." He waved his arm toward two wooden chairs that were slightly less scarred than the ones they had been sitting on in the hall. The deputy slouched into a chair next to the proffered ones and produced a tiny notebook from his shirt pocket.

"Deputy Swartz will stay and take a few notes for us, if you don't mind," Sheriff Knapp said.

Theodora assured the sheriff that the deputy's presence was appreciated. She thanked him politely for his time and smiled with a political mask that mirrored his.

The sheriff beamed back first at Theodora and then at Grace. He focused on Grace and his eyes narrowed almost imperceptibly. "And how is Mr. Shepard?" he said in a tone of voice that clearly implied "does your husband know you are here, little lady?"

"Mr. Shepard is fine, thank you sheriff. He sends his regards," Grace replied evenly. She did not take her eyes off of the sheriff's face and noticed his smile fade slightly then expand again like a piece of cracked china. Grace received the unspoken message that she had not responded quite meekly enough to suit him.

He straightened another pile of papers and leaned back on two legs of his chair. When he had his fingers laced casually across his ample belly, Sheriff Knapp looked up. The small talk was finished. The smiling facade had vanished, replaced by a sober expression. Grace sensed again that their visit was viewed as an irritating interruption. She twisted her mouth into what she hoped was a disarming smile and turned her head demurely in Theodora's direction.

Theodora paused a moment before relating the events leading to their suspicion that Will McClanahan was embezzling money from Lily Cross and her nephew, J.A. Simon. She forced her voice into the humble tone of a woman urgently requiring assistance, a woman who had come to the best man for the job.

Sheriff Knapp seemed to warm to her tone. He smiled benignly as she told the story, nodding his head in all the right places and murmuring "hm-m-m" and "uh-huh" to indicate that he was indeed listening carefully. Grace wondered if this was an election year.

Deputy Swartz did not take a single note and looked as though he might doze off at any moment. Scratching the swell of his stomach appeared to be the only activity that kept him awake in the warm room.

When Theodora finished, Sheriff Knapp leaned forward in his chair and picked up a pencil. Pointing it at Theodora, he said, "Sounds like a whole lot of speculation to me, ladies. Mr. Will McClanahan is a respected man in Benton Harbor, being the superintendent of public instruction and all. I personally know that all of the ownership papers on the opera house were filed properly. Place has been losing money for years. Miss Lily is lucky McClanahan bailed her out. I can't go nosing around in his personal matters just because he got himself into a fist fight with Evan Howell over a woman. Boys will be boys." He chuckled as if he had private knowledge of what they had been fighting about. From the lascivious grin on his face, Grace guessed that he had considered calling on Kathleen Carter himself.

"That opera house is a big place. Lots of expense. You ladies had no business snooping around in that office — McClanahan could have you cited for trespassing — but since you did," the sheriff said shaking his head, "I can only assume that you overlooked the charts that young Miss Emily Carter told you about. Mr. McClanahan is trying to rebuild a business that Miss Lily Cross and that nephew of hers let fall into ruin. Let's give him the benefit of the doubt, shall we?" Sheriff Knapp rose to his feet and moved toward the door with a forced show of hospitality. His speech patterns revealed him as a man educated in the school of hard knocks, albeit one who knew enough to act appropriately when the situation merited it. "Thank you for your time, ladies," he said with finality. "We always do appreciate the interest of our fine citizens."

Theodora did not protest. She glanced at Grace. There would be no help from the sheriff and it would be useless at this juncture to pursue his cooperation any further.

"It is late," Grace said when they left the station. "Do you want me to drop you at home?"

"I think I need look in on Miss Lily Cross, if you do not mind stopping there on your way home."

"Not at all, her house is right on my way. But I must get home, Helen feels she has been doing too much work lately and she is becoming increasingly irritated with me."

"I can walk home from Miss Lily's. It is a fine day and I need the time to think what to do next. It is obvious that Sheriff Knapp is not going to help us, at least not until we are able to provide more evidence. In fact, now that we have told him and Miss Emily what we think, Mr. McClanahan is very likely to find out about our suspicions. We shall need to be more careful and discreet, whatever course of action we decide to follow."

"It was worth a try in any case," Grace said. "The main thing is to help Miss Lily." She pulled Belle to a halt in front of the Cross house and Theodora held her skirts above her ankles and jumped to the ground.

On the short drive home, Grace mulled over the situation. What was Mr. McClanahan doing with Miss Lily's money? He and his wife lived in a modest house. Their children were adequately, but not expensively clothed. He had made no visible improvements on the opera house and certain areas were in deplorable condition. There was talk among the stage hands that the new-fangled electrical wiring had not been properly installed nor was it being maintained according to specifications.

Grace concluded her mental notations by resolving to secure some assistance for Miss Lily. Helping her was what Karla and Cynthia had been called here to do and Grace intended to follow through on that.

She forced herself — temporarily, at least — to forget about Mr. Will McClanahan and Sheriff Knapp and focus upon the problem at hand. It was obvious that Miss Lily was in need of live-in companionship which would undoubtably be difficult to obtain under the circumstances of her demanding behavior. The addition of one or more persons in the Cross household would eliminate the need for Mrs. McClanahan to prepare additional meals for Miss Lily which might serve to ease that unfortunate woman's situation as well. Grace sighed, there were so many needy people in this world. Treating everyone as if they were hurting seemed to be the best approach to life.

At home, Grace discussed Miss Lily's living conditions with Helen but did not divulge her suspicions regarding Mr. Will McClanahan. She and Theodora had decided that to spread such hearsay around town — especially in light of the sheriff's stubborn stance on the subject — would be foolhardy and would only serve to weaken their chances of thwarting him. As it was, Grace was convinced that the sheriff, and perhaps Miss Emily as well, would alert Mr. McClanahan to the fact that she and Theodora were asking questions concerning him and his business affairs.

Helen was shocked at Grace's description of Miss Lily's condition. "She has always been rather eccentric," Helen said. "But this is tragic. I feel simply terrible, I had no idea this was happening. Whoever will take care of Miss Lily? And the opera house, what will become of it? It is already in need of so many repairs. I assumed that Miss Lily was waiting for a break in the performance schedule or something of that nature. But I guess it has been years. Mercy me, the time goes by so quickly. Who will take charge of the opera house and care for it if Miss Lily cannot?"

Grace hesitated, then said, "Mr. Will McClanahan is the new owner of the opera house. He has been managing Miss Lily's affairs as they pertain to the theater. Mrs. Kathleen Carter sends her clothing and Mrs. McClanahan takes hot meals in to Miss Lily every day . . . " She let the sentence trail into thin air. I must be picking up Theodora's habits, Grace mused.

"Well, a man like that cannot be expected to know what is right for a lady Miss Lily's age. He has his hands full with that sickly wife of his and those children."

Helen stood up and began setting the table with a clatter of plates. She noisily selected enough silverware for their supper. Then, she said, "You say Mrs. McClanahan takes food to Miss Lily? I am flabbergasted she has enough fortitude to prepare meals at all the way she slumps around hanging her head like a whipped dog."

"I think Mr. McClanahan forces her do it."

"Whatever for?"

"As a way to protect his investment."

Helen looked puzzled.

Grace explained, "If he can keep Miss Lily in line — and in her house, out of his way — he can continue operating the theater without interference."

"Well, it sounds to me like someone had better interfere. What about that nephew of hers you mentioned, J.A. Simon? He works in the opera house. Unless someone stops him, that scoundrel McClanahan is going to ruin her family's business."

"That is just the problem Helen, it is no longer her concern. He has taken it clean away from her. It is all recorded neatly and legally at the courthouse. She could file charges against him, but as long as Miss Lily is convinced he is taking care of her personal interests, he is free to go about his business."

"I think I had best have a long talk with Miss Lily."

"I am certain she would enjoy a visit from you Helen, but for now she needs much more than visitors. She needs care. Will you assist me, Helen?"

Helen eagerly agreed to help and beamed a smile at Grace. This is a start, Grace thought. She was pleased with herself for reaching out to Helen. Everyone desires to be needed, and her mother-in-law was no exception.

Together, they prepared a list of potential women to serve as housemaids for Miss Lily. They decided that initially they would attempt to arrange a schedule of several women taking turns and continue on from there as the situation progressed.

❦ Chapter Thirteen

MISUSE OF MEDICATIONS

Lily Cross was outraged at the very idea of other women sharing her home. "I have to practice!" she raged. The lipstick smears on her face might have made her violent outbursts appear comical if she had not been so desperately serious.

"But Miss Lily," Grace said with a sudden flash of inspiration. "These women desire training in the theater, we thought if they could — "

"I cannot have people interrupting my work!" Lily insisted, throwing her head back so sharply Grace wondered that her neck did not snap.

"The ladies understand most completely that they may only observe you quietly from the background, not interfere at all. In exchange for your excellent example — mentoring of a sort — they would prepare meals for you, serve guests, perform light housekeeping and the like." Grace paused. She could see that Lily was softening to the idea. Her aura had turned from raging purple to a calming shade of lavender. "Miss Lily? How do you feel about this?" Grace said at last.

"I will consider it. Mentoring, you say?" Grace thought Lily said the word with a trace of awe in her tone. "I would be a mentor for these women? And what does that mean exactly?"

"Simply that they would observe your practicing and rehears-als in the hopes that they might absorb some of your immense talent. Perhaps sometimes, if you cared to, you might tell them something about life in the theater and your work. But only if that was what *you* desired. And of course, if it would not present an interruption to your work," Grace added quickly, hoping she had not flattered Miss Lily past the point of sincerity.

"Would they be asking questions?" Lily fluffed her hair into further disarray, nearly disheveling her small bun. She posed herself at the piano like a singer waiting for her cue.

"They might," Grace answered carefully. "But only if you felt the necessity of taking a pause from your practicing."

Lily swept the full skirt and petticoats she was wearing around to one side with an exaggerated gesture that nearly threw her off balance. She flounced down heavily on the piano stool.

The outdated clothing she wore contributed to her theatrical appearance as she sat with her back starchly erect and poised her bony fingers over the keyboard. Grace recognized snatches of Franz Liszt's "Hungarian Rhapsody No. 5" through Lily's deafening fumbling on the out-of-tune piano.

Lily ceased playing as suddenly as she had begun and abruptly turned to Grace. "I shall do it!" She exclaimed grandly. Her aura radiated like a lavender sunset around her face. She looked happy for the first time since Grace had begun visiting. "I owe it to the public, to my admirers. And besides, J.A. plans to present *The Factory Girl* in September. We will need several strong women to audition. Women of vision, as these women you are suggesting certainly must be if they wish to study under me."

"That is so very kind and generous of you, Miss Lily," Grace said. She was grateful for Lily's acceptance of the mentoring idea. Grace attributed this unexpected gift of psychological insight to Karla Cifelli. So often lately, Grace found herself saying just the right thing. She knew, however imperceptibly, that it was the work of Karla Cifelli who had entered her life so effortlessly. Now it was very nearly impossible to discern where Karla began and Grace Shepard ended. "I will bring some of the women over as soon as possible. May I go upstairs and prepare the bedrooms for their arrival? I must fetch clean linens, blankets and towels. Why, the water pitchers need filling ... there is really so much to be done in advance of their stay here."

"Certainly!" Lily shouted the word and pounded simultaneously on the keyboard.

As Grace walked up the staircase dustballs swirled around her skirts. In any case, a brisk and thorough cleaning will eliminate the litter and dirt that has been gathering in this house for far too long, Grace thought. She removed the coverlet from one bed and dust motes billowed from the fabric. This house needs a good airing out, Grace said to herself. She moved to open a window and looked down in time to see Will McClanahan coming across the yard carrying a covered tray.

Instinctively, Grace turned away from the glass. She stood very still to prevent the floor from creaking and listened as Will McClanahan entered the house without knocking. He called out for Lily and the screen door banged behind him. Grace tip-toed to the bedroom door but remained inside the room. She heard Mr. McClanahan tell Lily to eat all of her supper. His commanding voice caused Lily to stop playing and several minutes passed without a sound from below. Then Grace heard him tell Lily that she was a good girl. He marched through the pantry to the back of the house and banged the door closed again on his way out.

Grace gathered up the bed linens and walked quickly downstairs. A thick cloud of dust rose from the floor as she dropped the laundry in a pile near the front door. Grace brushed the dust from her dress and returned to the parlor.

Lily was wandering in a small circle around the piano.

"Miss Lily?" Grace said. She watched as Lily twirled around and rolled her eyes. She appeared to be dizzy and staggered toward the only chair left in the room.

Grace rushed to her side as Lily limply sank into the chair and promptly fainted. Grace was frantic. She reached for Lily's wrist and felt for a pulse. Lily's blood was racing, but the color had drained from her skin. Grace slapped Lily's face gently and then harder until Lily opened her eyes.

"Miss Lily?" Grace repeated. She held the woman's face in her hands and looked squarely into her eyes. Lily's pupils were dilated to the size of black marbles.

"I am going to rest now, I feel so very exhaus . . ." Lily said. The words muffled out as if her mouth was filled with cotton. Her head slumped over unnaturally to one side.

Grace quickly covered her with one of the dusty blankets from the hallway and dashed outside. She untied the reins and urged Belle down the driveway. As the carriage raced down Main Street, Grace prayed that Theodora would be in her office.

"Theo!" Grace called as she burst through the door. "Do come quickly, please. Something dreadful has happened to Miss Lily Cross."

Grace explained the situation as the two women drove east on Main Street toward the Cross house. Theodora listened intently. She clutched her leather doctor's bag with one hand and held onto the side of the carriage with the other. Grace leaned forward in the driver's seat as she urged Belle back toward Lily's yard.

Lily was snoring loudly when they entered the parlor. The wool blanket had slipped to the floor. Her legs were spread apart in a most ungainly and awkward position under her colorful layers of petticoats. Theodora made a cursory examination.

"She has been drugged," Theodora said.

"It had to be Mr. McClanahan's food," Grace said. "She was not in this condition before he walked over with the tray."

Together, Grace and Theodora lifted Lily by the arms and assisted her up the well-worn stairs and into her sitting room.

Lily nodded in and out of a heavy sleep and muttered unintelligibly as they placed her on the fainting couch, undressed her, and covered her with a quilt. Grace picked up the pile of soiled clothing as Theodora pulled the dark, cambric shades. They quietly left the room.

"We should thoroughly search the rooms downstairs to be certain Miss Lily is not hiding anything that she could have ingested herself while you were up here earlier." Theodora suggested.

"That will not be difficult. With all of the furnishings Miss Lily has been burning, there are not too many hiding places left."

They carefully canvassed the first level of the house and found nothing except one half empty bottle of sherry. Grace perused the many bookshelves in the library with an interest she could not remember feeling before Karla entered her life. While thumbing through the untouched pages for packets of powder or cutout hiding places, she was unable to stop herself from drifting into the printed words on the pages. She found the firmness of the paper, the delicate script and the musty smell of trapped wisdom within the books entrancing. It was with concerted effort that she replaced each book in its row on the shelves and selected another to check for hidden medications.

One gilded volume was entitled *The Gargoyles of New York*. Grace admired the elaborate embossing as she turned the book to open it. It fell open to a page that had been read so many times the binding was cracked at its place. The page was dog-earred and several passages were underlined. Grace began reading:

> *Gargoyle, in architecture, a decorated waterspout often made of terra-cotta or wood carved to resemble grotesque lions or other beasts. The Gothic gargoyle is usually a frightening bird or beast sitting on its haunches on the back of a cornice moulding. May be constructed more elaborately of precious metals and stones such as the type found on the Farmers Loan and Trust building in New York City. (see illustration, next page)*

Grace turned the page to an illustrated series of eight gargoyles. One, the detail of the Farmers Loan and Trust building, was marked with a handwritten notation, which read "1860, M. Cross."

Grace studied the drawing. It reminded her of something. "Theodora look here," she said. "Is this gargoyle the same as the ones decorating either side of the stage at the Yore Opera House?"

Theodora looked at the page as Grace handed her the open book. "Could be," she said. "It is difficult to recall. The theater is usually so dark when I am seated there, and my thoughts tend to wander. I think I must have glanced at them a hundred times, but I truly cannot be certain. Why do you ask?"

"I am not sure. A notation on the previous page, I have a hunch that there might be something more to this."

The women concluded their search for drugs in the kitchen. Lily Cross kept very little in her larder. The plain, painted shelves were fairly bare but for a crock of pickles, assorted jars of candied watermelon and pickled corn. One sack of wheat flour had tiny black insects crawling among the grains. A couple of cones of white sugar were crispy and yellow for want of use. Much of the once fine china was now chipped and cracked, all of it layered thickly with dust. A higher shelf displayed a set of Spode china in a delicate blue and white flowered pattern. It, too, was caked with oil and dust.

"I doubt very much that Miss Lily has been drugging herself," Grace said, "although she does display a fondness for sherry. This kitchen, however, appears to be largely unused."

"I agree. There is nothing here," Theodora said reluctantly, wiping her hands on a faded and frayed linen dish towel. "The pain killers which I prescribe can cause the symptoms exhibited by Miss Lily when too many are ingested, especially when they are mixed with alcohol. Sometimes the heavy sleep is just what the doctor ordered, but it appears Miss Lily has been overdosed. And that explains why Mrs. McClanahan's medicine disappears so often."

"Do you think he steals it from her?"

"Most probably, and it would be just like him to accuse his hapless wife of misplacing it. I would like to get both Miss Lily and Mrs. McClanahan out from under his dominating manner. How is this business of the housekeepers for Miss Lily progressing?"

"Helen and I have a couple of excellent possibilities from church. There are apparently some ladies in unfortunate straits who might also benefit from such an arrangement. Under the circumstances, I shall stay the night myself. Miss Lily is sleeping soundly now, but I do not wish for her to be alone when she awakens."

"We need to confront Mr. Will McClanahan as soon as possible," Theodora said. Her clear blue eyes expanded with conviction. "He cannot continue this cruel abuse of Miss Lily with drugs and intimidation. It might be too late to get the opera house back for her — although I certainly intend to try — but we *can* reclaim her dignity. If not her very life!"

❦ Chapter Fourteen

A CONFRONTATION

When Theodora and Grace walked into Will McClanahan's office the next day, he stood up indignantly. The top of his massive oak desk was covered with disheveled piles of papers that merged into one malignant heap. The room was dusty and gas sconces cast a dim glow over the disorder. Grace felt a surge of pity for the hapless pupils who entered this loathsome office for this man's disciplinary recourse.

"Do you have an appointment?" he demanded. From his hostile tone, Grace guessed that he was aware of their investigation.

"It is most unlikely that we will require an appointment when you find out what we have to say to you," Theodora said evenly. She looked him directly in the eye and advanced toward his desk.

He stood his ground, but Grace noticed his eyes narrow into slits under the shadow of the grey emanation which surrounded him. It had to be the nastiest aura Grace had ever observed.

"Well, do get to the point then, I have much to accomplish prior to the start of school in September." He quickly consulted his pocket watch and walked to the back of the worn leather chair behind his desk. He placed his hands on its back and pinched the creased leather so hard his knuckles turned white.

"The point is," Theodora said. "We know what you have been doing to Miss Lily Cross and we want it to stop immediately."

"And what is that, pray tell?"

"Why, stealing the opera house from her for one thing."

"That is most absurd. I paid a just and fair amount for the purchase of that opera house and saved Miss Lily from a most unfortunate debt with the city. It is all accurately recorded at the courthouse."

"It is not all recorded, and we are certain that the papers are not accurate. Where do you keep the charts showing the walk- in traffic for performances?"

"I have no idea what you're talking about — " He answered so quickly his speech slurred and the contraction slipped out in the manner common to uneducated Victorian men. He was getting sloppy. Theodora took the opportunity to cut him off and rattle him further.

"The charts you keep separate from the reserved seating. Where does all of that money go? Let me tell you where it goes, Mr. Will McClanahan. It goes to Mrs. Kathleen Carter and not for her acting prowess either. We have become alerted to the fact that she has been blackmailing you, and we suspect that it has been occuring ever since she first arrived here in Benton Harbor. A grave burden upon you to be sure, but one that gives you motive to take advantage of poor Miss Lily." Theodora spoke in a low voice, enunciating her words carefully so Will McClanahan could clearly hear her, but the conversation would not carry out of the closed office to the ears of the secretary in the outer room.

"That is quite enough!" McClanahan exploded. "Get out of my office or I'll . . . I will send for the sheriff and have you re-moved. This visit is laughable and insulting." He walked piously from behind the desk but caught his foot on the edge of the rug and stumbled as he headed toward the door.

We have shaken his guard, Grace thought, observing his reactions. This is a man who will indeed make mistakes.

"I hardly think the townspeople would find it laughable that their superintendent of public instruction was supporting an illegitimate child with funds, ah . . . shall we say embezzled — however skillfully you have concealed it — from poor Miss Lily Cross."

"Good day, Dr. Goodhart. Mrs. Shepard. I think I have en-dured quite enough of your ridiculous and most irritating accusa-tions for one morning."

"I have seen Miss Emily Carter's birth certificate in Detroit, Mr. McClanahan." Theodora said firmly.

Grace dared not make a move. She knew Theodora was bluffing and prayed fervently that Will McClanahan could not look through her skin and see her heart pounding into her throat.

McClanahan stopped dead in his tracks. Theodora Goodhart,

a medical doctor, would have access to such records. Her unshakable confidence was indeed convincing. Grace wondered if the certificate still existed. She guessed that Will McClanahan was pondering the same question. It would be just the sort of trick Kathleen Carter would hold in abeyance until she needed it.

Grace ventured a look in McClanahan's direction. His aura had turned murky and black like a death shroud hanging over his shoulders. She could see that he was struggling with this new piece of information. His jowls sagged as he turned toward Theodora, but his black eyes burned with hatred.

"You're lying!" he shouted.

"Am I indeed?"

"What exactly do you intend to prove by dragging my name through public disgrace and humiliation? I have a family. Innocent children are involved, including Miss Emily Carter. Is it your wish for her to become the target of malicious back room gossip?

"And you, Mrs. Shepard. Is the good Mr. Shepard aware that you spend your days idly poking around in other people's business affairs? He should give you a good strapping."

"Is that how you solve your problems, Mr. McClanahan? With the leather strap?"

Grace thought of Hilda McClanahan's stooped posture and of the cuts and bruises she had witnessed on Kathleen Carter's fragile, battered body.

"I'll thank you to keep your accusations to yourself. How I solve my problems is my business not yours. Now if there is nothing further, you will please excuse me. I have an appointment I must keep."

"When did you begin administering drugs to Miss Lily Cross?" Theodora said, stepping into his path.

"Get out!" McClanahan pushed past Theodora and opened the door. "If I hear of any more probing accusations from you trifling women, I will have the sheriff lock up both of you and throw away the key!"

His aura flamed in jagged edges around his body. It was clear to Grace that his was a rage that could break out of control at any moment. She took Theodora's arm and steered her forcibly out the door.

"Good day, Mr. McClanahan." Grace said starchly. Then, gulping down her fear of him, she turned and said, "See that you stay away from Miss Lily Cross. She will no longer be requiring meals or any other type of assistance from you or Mrs. McClanahan."

A blast of air caught Grace's skirt lifting it above her ankles as he slammed the door behind them. The school secretary looked up in surprise as the door frame rattled and the women quickly exited.

"Someone ought to medicate him," Theodora said indignantly when they were outside. Then, slowly, a smirk crossed her face that could only have come from the twentieth century.

The part of Grace that was influenced by Karla Cifelli recognized the look. Cynthia Marigold's bold personality was alive and well within the body of Dr. Theodora Goodhart.

"I think we pushed him as far as was prudent," Grace said cautiously. "When a man like Will McClanahan is backed into a corner, anything can happen. Murderous thoughts, even killing could happen, Theodora. We have placed him into the position of protecting his own territory, at least territory that he perceives as under his ownership. I shudder to think what a man with that kind of rage might do next."

"That is true," Theodora said. "Any man — or woman for that matter — is capable of killing if pushed far enough or frightened."

Theodora was silent for a moment. Her eyes widened with determination. "It is time, I feel, to place a circle of protection around Miss Lily," she said. "He has been drugging her to keep her subdued and quiet and to keep her under his control. Might you possibly get away again tonight?"

"Yes, I think so. But why do you say he needs to keep her quiet? Whatever do you think she knows that he would have need to suppress?"

"I am not sure, perhaps something about the opera house," Theodora said. She climbed into the passenger side of Grace's carriage and thumped down angrily on the wooden seat.

Leaving the school, they had to pass by the opera house at the corner of Sixth and Territorial. Grace steered Belle to the side of

91

the building and pulled the carriage to a halt. Belle moved to a clump of weeds and nibbled on the greenery interspersed among the careless clutter of paper, string and rotting debris in the street.

A few people were working on the stage when Grace and Theodora entered the theater. Empty places where four gargoyles had hung stood out amid elaborate decorations at either side of the stage. Closer scrutiny revealed several holes in the wall where the inanimate beasts had been affixed to the wooden surface with bolts.

"The gargoyles are gone," Grace said. "Someone has removed them. See the bolt holes where they were? I feel certain that the gargoyle in the book is the same as the ones that were placed here for ornamentation."

"Would Miss Lily remember exactly what was here?"

"Good question," Grace replied. "People — especially older people, like Miss Lily — tend to remember the past better than they might recall what happened to them yesterday. Perhaps we will learn the answer tonight."

CHAPTER FIFTEEN

A RITUAL OF PROTECTION

Grace quickly packed a basket of breads, jellies, chicken and fruit that Helen had prepared for supper into the back of the buggy. Wedging extra jars of preserves next to the basket, she was careful not to crush three tightly wrapped plates of cakes and cookies. Snugging a jug of hot coffee in at the last, Grace covered it all with a fur throw and climbed into the driver's seat. She flicked the reins with a light touch and Belle sauntered out of the curving drive onto Territorial Road and trotted down the hill toward town.

Driving past the Yore Opera House on the way to Miss Lily's house, Grace stared up at the four-story building. Four gargoyles had been an integral part of the stage's elaborate ornamentation. How long had they been missing? It had to be Will McClanahan who had removed them or ordered their removal, Grace reasoned, and she guessed that they had not been gone too long. Someone would have noticed their absence. It seemed likely that he had either sold them off or, hopefully, had them hidden somewhere inside the opera house.

Theodora was already inside with Miss Lily when Grace arrived at the Cross home. She carried the basket of supper — baked chicken still warm from the oven, biscuits and breads with sweet butter, strawberry preserves, apricot cookies and Helen's special Shepard cake — into the kitchen. Theodora had washed and dried a pan full of dishes and was setting the dining room table while Miss Lily looked on and chattered happily. Grace was pleased to see her looking so well. Miss Lily's color was good and she appeared more alert than she had been in weeks. Grace laid out the light supper on a tray and put the coffee on the stove to reheat.

"Does Miss Lily have any dining room chairs left?" Grace asked as she entered the room where Theodora was just finishing

93

with the table service. Grace placed the tray on the buffet where Miss Lily was earnestly polishing a silver coffee pot and getting more fingerprints on it than off; but no matter Grace thought, at least she was trying to help.

Theodora glanced around the nearly barren room. "It seems we may need to bring in benches from the kitchen," she concluded, then added, "Miss Lily wanted to dine in here because we are her most special guests."

"Why thank you, Miss Lily," Grace said.

"Well, you are you know," Lily declared shyly. "You both are most definitely my dearest guests."

"Miss Lily," Grace said, "do you remember the gargoyles on either side of the stage inside the opera house?"

"Oh yes," Lily replied. "They were my grandfather's pride and joy. He brought them here years ago from New York. They were reproductions of some sort. He was so happy when Father purchased the opera house that he would have a proper place to display them. He always said they were important works of art with their wooden carvings and all."

"Would they have been very valuable, do you think?"

"Grandfather seemed to think so, he always said they were the icing on the cake."

"Valuable enough for someone to want to steal them?"

"Oh, they could never be stolen. How could they be? They are up so high, someone would have to have access to ladders; besides, they are bolted to the columns." Lily finished the chicken leg she had snatched from the tray and tossed the bone toward the fireplace missing the grate by two feet. She picked up another piece with her fingers and gnawed on it thoughtfully. "You know," she continued, "before his death, grandfather started insisting that the gargoyles were filled with gold. Father and I never believed him. He tended to make up stories. You know how older folk can go on endlessly sometimes."

Grace shot Theodora a meaningful look. "Did you ever come to tell the McClanahans this story?" Grace asked Lily.

"I might have. He was always asking me questions about the opera house." Lily tossed the second bone at the fireplace. This time it bounced off of the hearth and skittered back across the once lovely dining room floor.

Grace remembered the room as it had been just after Mr. Cross' funeral. The ornate furnishings had been elegantly set off by a large Persian rug and the crystal chandelier which still hung from the center of the ceiling. Whatever could have happened to the rug, Grace wondered? Surely, Miss Lily would not have burned it?

Lily yawned. "I am so dreadfully sleepy these days," she said stretching her arms above her head. "I believe I will go upstairs and take a light rest."

Theodora spoke up quickly. "Oh, please Miss Lily, do let me pour you a nice cup of coffee. There is a matter of great importance that we need to discuss with you."

Lily looked interested. "You young ladies are so much more cordial to me than Mr. McClanahan. Why he never dined with me, you know," Lily said. "He simply stood over me like a soldier, insisting that I clean my plate so he could return it to Mrs. McClanahan, and he never bothered so much as to answer a query of mine after I sold the opera house to him. Someone told me about men like him. Now who had that been? And why had I not listened?" Lily twisted her hair between her greasy fingers and scuffed at the floor with one foot.

"We are going to stay the night with you, Miss Lily, and when we leave tomorrow, you must promise never to take any more food from Mr. Will McClanahan or Mrs. McClanahan," Grace said. She kept her eyes firmly locked on Lily's. "Please do not accept further gifts of food or clothing from Miss Kathleen Carter or Miss Emily Carter."

"Try to prevent any of them from entering this house. I want you to keep the doors and windows bolted from the inside. Is that understood, Miss Lily?" Theodora added.

Lily nodded and took a sip of the strong coffee. She nibbled absently on a piece of lemon bread which crumbled into her lap. "May I inquire as to why?" she asked. "He has promised to cast me in the leading role of *The Factory Girl*. It will be our next show. I have my heart quite set upon the role, you know."

"Mr. Will McClanahan has been feeding you medications in the food he brings over here, Miss Lily. That is why you always fall asleep after supper."

Lily looked like a puzzled child. In her outdated clothing and smudgy make-up, she managed to maintain a girlish demeanor despite her years.

"Believe me, Miss Lily. I am a doctor and I assure you that the heavy sleep which you have become accustomed to after supper is induced by some particular medications. They cause you to become both sick and moonish. Mrs. Shepard and I are going to help you regain your vigor and strength but you need to stay away from Mr. and Mrs. McClanahan."

"He has been awfully rude lately," Lily admitted. "But I do try to remain on the good side of him in order to reserve my status on the stage." She looked doubtful.

"It is prudent policy to attempt to remain on the good side of people whenever possible Miss Lily. But Mr. McClanahan has been harming you. Since we do not have sufficient evidence for the sheriff, it is best to avoid him."

"The sheriff?" Miss Lily asked.

"Well, yes," Theodora said. She was not certain how much of this matter Miss Lily needed to know for her own safety. "You do understand that he has been medicating the food he brings here for you?"

"I suppose so." Miss Lily looked back and forth from Theodora to Grace.

"And you know that you must not eat any more of his food?"

"Yes." Lily sounded more certain on this point. Theodora decided to forge ahead.

"Good. Mrs. Shepard and I have reason to suspect that Mr. McClanahan has been stealing from you and your family since he has been keeping your books. That is why the opera house has lost so much money."

"There might be money in the opera house?" Miss Lily sat up straight. All thought of sleep had vanished from her mind.

"It is very likely."

"Why that scoundrel, Will McClanahan!"

Grace decided that now was as good a time as any to get to the purpose of the evening.

"With your permission, we would like to perform a ritual of

protection around you and your home, Miss Lily. We believe it will help you to keep Mr. McClanahan at bay," Grace said. She studied Lily's expression in order to gauge her reaction to the suggestion of a ritual held outside of a church. Some local citizens, Grace knew, felt that the practice was ineffective.

She need not have worried. Lily's eyes widened over the coffee cup. She put it down on the table with a clatter, sloshing some of the brown liquid into the saucer in her haste. Her rouged cheeks glowed with excitement.

Lily exclaimed, "A ritual! Smashing idea! I cannot recall anyone suggesting such a thing since Mrs. Lincoln was in the White House."

She looked from Grace to Theodora. "Oh, of course, you girls are far too young to remember the seances she held there back in the sixties." Lily leaned forward and whispered, "Word was that he, Mr. Lincoln that is, participated, too, although he never admitted it publicly."

"Mr. Lincoln was ahead of his time in many ways."

"It was quite the talk of the town, if not the country. Now that we have that dull Presbyterian Cleveland in office, nothing ever happens." Lily pushed away from the table and wiped the chicken grease from her hands onto her skirt narrowly missing the crumpled silk clusters of bows sewn at both sides.

Grace handed Lily a tray and said in a gentle voice, "Very good. Before we begin, will you help me gather the dishes, please Miss Lily?"

When they moved to the kitchen, Theodora placed a cloth bag of sage on the table and wiped the dust from one of the cast iron frying pans with a kitchen rag. She rubbed the dry sage leaves between her palms letting the pieces fall into the pan. When the dishes were finished and the pan was full of sage, the three women went into the garden and viewed the waxing moon.

"I call upon the moon to protect this house," Theodora said softly, holding the skillet of sage to the sky in a graceful gesture.

Lily stared at the moon, her face beaming with pleasure. She seemed to understand these early elements of the ritual. Grace wondered if perhaps Miss Lily herself had participated in such activities during the 1860s and if the events of this evening were bringing back the memories.

Grace took Lily's hand and they returned through the back porch to the kitchen. Theodora lit the sage and fanned the flame causing smoke to rise from the pan. Holding the pan in one hand and lightly fanning the smoking sage with the other, Theodora walked three times in a clockwise direction around Lily. She recited a brief chant about safety, long life and continued protection. Lily clapped her hands together and fairly danced with delight.

Then, Theodora lit four white candles, and as she handed two of the candles to Grace, and two to Lily, she called upon the directions of north, south, east and west — the four corners of the universe — to avail themselves of safe places on Miss Lily's behalf. Grace and Lily held the candles in front of their bodies so that their faces glowed in the soft light. Grace thought that Miss Lily had never looked prettier.

They followed along with the candles as Theodora circled each room in the house three times, pushing smoke with her hand into every corner and crevice. She paid special attention to each window and door, fanning the smoke over and around them with her hand. When they had traveled throughout the house, Theodora opened the front and back doors, letting the wind blow the smoke through the house, cleansing it.

Lily watched with uncontained excitement. "May I do it?" she asked Theodora.

"Of course, Miss Lily," Theodora answered in a patient voice. "We need to add more sage and go outside."

On the back porch, Theodora instructed Lily to fan smoke around the doorway and down the steps to the yard. As they walked clockwise around the house, Theodora carried the two candles and recited something that sounded like poetry to Grace even though it did not rhyme. The cadence of her words kept their feet together as the women walked three times around Lily's house. All the while Lily giggled as she fanned the smoke with her free hand.

"You did an excellent job, Miss Lily," Theodora said when they were back inside the kitchen. She left the remaining sage in the skillet to burn itself out, and placed the candle pieces on a small square of cloth. To finish the ritual, Theodora would cast all of the leftovers into the St. Joseph River at her earliest opportunity.

"The hour is growing late, we can retire to bed now, if you like, Miss Lily," Grace suggested.

"Tell me a story first," Lily whined like a petulant child.

"All right, but first you must get into bed. I do not want you falling asleep in the chair if my story gets too long and boring."

"Your stories could not possibly be boring," Lily said sincerely.

They climbed the stairs to Lily's bedroom. When she was settled under the coverlet, Grace began speaking in a voice so soothing, Theodora almost fell asleep listening to her. Lily nodded and struggled to keep awake during Grace's story, but residue from the excessive medications she had ingested lingered in her system and she fell quickly asleep.

"Theodora," Grace whispered when they were back downstairs. "Did you notice the lights on in McClanahan's house when we were outside? I saw him walk by the window once so I know he is in there. I want to get inside the opera house and look for the gargoyles. I have a hunch they are hidden inside."

"You do not mean to break in at this hour?"

"Well, not break in, no. But perhaps a door or a window has been carelessly left open."

Theodora tilted her head toward Grace.

"I feel certain that there is something about those gargoyles that we need to know, Theodora. Maybe there is gold inside of them as Miss Lily said. We cannot afford to wait too long or Mr. McClanahan might make off with the treasure."

"If there is any."

"It seems likely that there is, otherwise why would he have removed all of them? I can see removing one or two just to look, but if they were empty, why would he bother to go further with such a dangerous job?"

"Greed?"

"Well, he is greedy, yes. And he completely defaced those columns. So the gargoyles must be worth something. Even if they are empty, maybe the carvings are valuable and we can sell them for money for Miss Lily. In any case, I am outside of the house for this evening. I cannot make excuses to Dan and Helen indefinitely."

Theodora thought for a moment, then said, "I have some candles and matches in my bag. We do not need the risk of turning on the lights and having someone walk by and see us there."

"It is just one street over, we can cut through the orchard and be there in no time."

Grace went upstairs to check on Lily. She was snoring soundly. Grace adjusted the coverlet more snugly around Lily and closed the bedroom door on her way out.

The two women walked quietly through Lily's back yard and past the McClanahan's house. All of the lights were extinguished.

"They look to all be asleep," Grace whispered.

Theodora cast her eyes toward the waxing moon. She said, "We are well protected for this evening, I think."

❦ Chapter Sixteen

EVENTS AT THE YORE OPERA HOUSE

Their long dresses rustled and tangled as they hurried through the fruit trees toward the corner of Sixth and Territorial where the four-story building made an impressive silhouette against the darkened sky.

At the opera house, they walked into the alleyway at the back of the building. Grace tried to budge the heavy sash on one of the windows. It was locked. She moved quickly along the side of the building, carefully avoiding snagging her skirts on the rough bricks. She reached the next window and tried it. This one opened easily into the basement. Theodora held the window up while Grace struggled inside and dropped to the floor below. With some difficulty, she was able to push herself through the small window despite the cumbersome length of her skirt.

"You can manage it," Grace said to Theodora who was surveying the tiny opening with a look of skepticism on her face.

Inside, Grace found a crate and used it as a step to reach the window. She propped the window open with a stick. Theodora passed her bag to Grace. Securing her long skirt with one hand, Theodora barely managed to squeeze through the basement window to the dirt floor below.

"If I gain so much as a pound while we are in here, I will not make it back out of that window," Theodora said brushing the dust from her skirt.

Using the light from the moon, the women adjusted their eyes and surveyed the musty, cluttered basement. It was stacked to the rafters with furniture and properties from past productions. Some of the pieces were covered with old sheets giving the crowded basement a ghostly air.

"I do not even know where to begin," Theodora said, pulling a candle from her bag and handing it to Grace.

"Hide in plain sight is our motto, right?" Grace replied with confidence instilled by Karla Cifelli. She lit her stubby candle from the flame burning on Theodora's wick and cautiously moved forward into the obstructed room.

She peered under sheets and into the vast assortment of bulky steamer trunks. Tangles of electrical wiring hung in messy bunches from the rafters. She wished they dared pull the chain on the light bulb she noticed hanging from one snarl of wiring.

"Grace, look here," Theodora said with a triumphant tone. "You clever girl, see what I have found sitting smack in the middle of the room."

Grace hurried over, weaving among the trunks and boxes, to where Theodora was standing and held her candle above the yawning mouths of four carved wooden gargoyles.

"One is sawed in half," she said easily lifting one half of the beastly carving. "The inside is hollow."

Theodora bent down slowly, keenly aware — as she often was — that the latest fashion in dresses did not make for comfortable movements. She attempted to pick up another one of the beasts. It would not budge. "I fear this one is far too heavy for me to move," Theodora said.

"Then it must be filled with something. This half of one is of fairly light weight," Grace said putting the hollow half down and trying without success to lift a whole gargoyle. "Might there be a saw down here?" she suggested.

"Goodness Grace, you surely are becoming too bold for words," Theodora said looking around for a saw. "I did notice a workbench against that wall. Just a minute."

When Theodora returned to the gargoyles with a sturdy handsaw, Grace fixed her candle to the floor with a small pool of beeswax and took the saw from Theodora. She began a rhythmic sawing motion at the narrowest diameter of the gargoyle's neck. Within minutes, its head fell off and coins of gold spilled to the floor.

"Mercy me, Theodora. This is a fortune! We must find something strong enough to carry these coins out."

They filled Theodora's bag as well as three smaller canvas bags they discovered among the costumes in the basement. As the contents of the gargoyle grew smaller they were able to lift it enough to spill out all of the coins onto the floor.

"I want every one of these coins for Miss Lily," Grace said. "Mr. Will McClanahan shall not get his hands on another cent."

"Hear, hear," Theodora said filling the last bag and carrying it to the window. She returned the saw to the work bench and hurried back to the gargoyles where Grace was sweeping the telltale sawdust underneath a chest of drawers.

"We need to erase these broom tracks and pick up the broken straw as well," Grace said stamping her feet over the places she had swept on the dirt floor. Theodora joined her and when they were satisfied that the area looked as it had before their arrival, she pieced the gargoyle together and set it aside.

"At least he will not notice the missing coins at first glance," Grace said surveying their work. As a final touch, she tossed a lace glove from one of the costumes onto the floor near the gargoyles.

Grace crawled through the window and crouched in the alley, reaching back into the opening as Theodora handed out the four heavy bags of coins. "I pray that no one sees us. How would we ever explain our presence in town at this late hour?" she whispered as Theodora struggled through the window. Helping Theodora to her feet, Grace reached down and pulled the window closed.

"If anyone spies us, we simply remain silent and keep walking," Theodora said. "Hide in plain sight, remember? Where did you get that notion anyway?"

"Why, from you of course. The last time we entered this opera house uninvited."

"Oh, yes. You are quite right, Grace. So much has happened, I had forgotten that incident. Please accept my apologies."

"Certainly, Theodora."

They scanned the alleyway in both directions before picking up the bags and holding their skirts in the same grasp. The heavy bags hung in the folds of their generous garments as the women moved silently away from the building. A soft rustling of fabric

103

was all that could be heard as they walked. It was dark, but the waxing moon illuminated even the shadowy corners of the alley. There was no one else in sight.

"What are we going to do with these bags?" Grace asked. "Mr. McClanahan has access to Miss Lily's house and we cannot take them to mine with all of the children and Helen there. Would you have any place that might be secure enough to store them until we decide what to do?"

They walked south on Sixth, turning west at Main Street in the direction of Theodora's house. The weight of the gold forced them to let go of their skirts in order to manage the heavy bags hanging at their sides. The long skirts tangled around their ankles, hindering the pace of their steps.

"You know, I think I do have a place that would be secure," Theodora said after a bit. "Remember the indoor plumbing that Mr. Ferris was installing in my kitchen before he died — God rest his soul. He never completed the work, poor thing, so I have this large drain pipe extending from underneath my wash basin, where he was intending to install a sink. It leads underground a short way almost to the lilac bushes, but I do think there is enough room for the coins."

Lily was breathing deeply when Grace and Theodora peered through her doorway. It was almost dawn. Pink light edged the orchards to the east of the Cross house. The night air had been cool and still. Grace could feel its glow on her cheeks.

"Sleeping like a baby," Grace whispered.

"We should be, too," Theodora said doubtfully, "but I feel a bit too anxious for sleep." She motioned toward the stairs and the women quietly descended.

In the kitchen, the stove door creaked at its rusty places as Grace opened it to stoke the fire with twigs. She ground some fresh beans and put a pot of coffee on to boil before adding a log to the stove. Wiping her hands on a faded towel, Grace turned to where Theodora was sitting at the long wooden table.

"Miss Lily needs more kindling," Grace said absently.

"Miss Lily has need of many things that that gold can buy her. Grace, we have to get the rest of it out of there as soon as we possibly can. When Mr. McClanahan finds out that some of it is

104

missing, we will be suspect and there is no telling what a man such as he might do. We have him fairly backed into a corner, and cornered men fight for their freedom."

The coffee started boiling and its enameled pot moved with an insistent clatter on the cast iron stove. Grace rinsed and dried two of Miss Lily's dusty cups and saucers, the delicate Spode underscoring the wealth Miss Lily and her family had once owned.

Grace had not known the Cross family well, they had been absorbed with the workings of the opera house, and she had been busy raising her children. Grace remembered attending many benefit performances — sometimes with Dan on evening occasions, and often with the older children at matinee programs — that the Cross family had generously organized to raise money for charitable causes. The Cross name was highly revered by many in Benton Harbor who remembered those social events as part of what had allowed the city to prosper and to take care of its less able citizens as well. Unfortunately, thought Grace, Mr. Will McClanahan had little respect for the benevolent deeds of the past or the civic-minded people who orchestrated them.

Grace wondered when he had started embezzling the Cross family money? Miss Lily had been active on the stage when the McClanahans had arrived in town, and still later, when Kathleen followed them with his illegitimate daughter. It was not too long after Kathleen began working at the opera house that Miss Lily had retreated from acting. Had he or Kathleen begun taking advantage of her with drugs and intimidation as long ago as that?

Grace brought the cups to the table and stared into the middle distance. When had Miss Lily taken to her house? Try as she might, Grace was unable to pinpoint that time period; she had become so involved with the younger children as they came along that she had removed herself from most of Benton Harbor's social circles. Even in church, Grace had not found the time to converse with the other women who might have noticed Miss Lily's absence from the stage and subsequently from the business and the outside world. Had the absence been sudden or gradual?

Kathleen's rise as a leading lady on the Yore Opera House stage had been quite rapid, Grace recalled. Had Kathleen's abrupt rise to prominence and her outrageous behavior overshadowed Miss Lily's reclusive disappearance? Kathleen's outspoken opinions, her unconventional hairstyle, the heavy make-up and imprudent show of cleavage even in daytime, the pretentious construction of her mansion, her overt flirtations with married men, oh, the list goes on and on Grace thought. While Kathleen's behavior had occupied the wagging tongues of Benton Harbor, Miss Lily's misfortune had been allowed to slip away into obscurity.

"I think we must return tonight," Grace said snapping out of her reverie and fixing her eyes on Theodora. When their eyes met, Grace thought for a moment that she visualized eye beams like threads of light running between them. But when she blinked and stared again, the beams were gone. She took a sip of the steaming coffee and thought of the hot muffins that Helen was probably removing from the oven at this very moment.

"Dan and Helen are understanding of the necessity of my staying with Miss Lily, so I have a good reason to be out again this evening. What do you say, Theodora?"

Theodora looked appreciatively at her friend.

"I feel we should most definitely go tonight. Any postponement increases the danger of Mr. McClanahan learning of his losses, and," Theodora paused, searching for the proper words. "instigating further unethical actions."

"Let him try," Grace said with a vengeance that surprised her. She raised her eyebrows in an expression of amazement at her own heightened emotions and, in a subdued, apologetic tone, said, "I guess we all have a bit of the beast within us when it comes to protecting those we care about."

"That is so, Grace. That is so."

They clinked their china cups together and sipped a silent toast to the success of their mission.

That day was the longest one Grace could remember. She napped fitfully and fretted about Will McClanahan and his notoriously violent temper. That evening, after Miss Lily was comfortably tucked into her large Eastlake bed, Grace and Theodora lingered a little while longer. Theodora burned sage leaves in a dish and slowly inhaled the fragrant smoke.

They had gathered several canvas drawstring bags to carry the coins and another stick to prop the window. When the hour was right, they slipped out through the foyer door and cut across the orchard to Territorial Road. Having decided to leave their lanterns behind, Grace and Theodora stepped carefully, avoiding dirt clods and holes that might turn their ankles, and holding their long skirts above the ground as best they could.

Hugging closely to the empty office buildings, they passed by the Thayer Company and the Hotel Benton without notice. Even Schuder & Stein's saloon appeared empty of patrons as they crept along the downtown streets toward the corner of Territorial and Sixth.

Entering the alley behind the opera house, both women stopped short. There was a dim light shining from inside the basement into the dark alley. They slowly approached the window, surreptitiously stooping down and peering carefully through the wavy glass. The window was slightly ajar and the sound of metal grinding on wood drifted to them before they viewed the scene inside.

Mr. Will McClanahan was bent over, intently sawing one of the gargoyles in half. His back was to them. Neither woman dared to speak, and Grace could surely feel the utter disappointment that hung as heavy as a millstone in the space between them.

They were clearly no match for Mr. Will McClanahan's physical strength. By legal rights, he now owned the opera house and everything in it. There was nothing they could do but return to Miss Lily's house.

Grace quietly gathered her skirt and started to rise from her crouched position in the alley when a door banged from somewhere above, causing her to cringe back, pressing herself against the rough bricks of the building.

Kathleen Carter marched down the steep basement staircase, the French heels of her shoes snapping sharply against the wooden risers. Both Grace and Theodora moved quickly to the outer edge of the window frame, out of view, but well within earshot.

"So it is here that I find you, Will McClanahan!" Kathleen

107

shouted. "And to think I was expecting you this evening."

"As I told you, Kathleen, those meddling women are on to us. We are not safe right now. We should not be seen together, even here," he said, hastily standing up in an attempt to hide the gargoyles with his stance. He had gotten one of the wooden carvings sawed completely through, but the gold coins had not spilled out onto the dirt floor of the cluttered basement.

"Ha! How can you summon the nerve to imply that we might be discovered here, especially at this hour? As a matter of fact, Mr. Will McClanahan, I seem to recall many late hours when you could not wait to meet me here and to walk with me to my dressing room sofa. If we are not safe here, in the shelter of this basement, then where might we be safe?" Kathleen pointed accusingly at him, advancing menacingly in his direction.

Will moved to keep his body between Kathleen and the gargoyles.

"Whatever are you hiding back there?" she said stepping to the side to see what was behind him.

"Absolutely nothing."

"Then move over."

"It is my business."

"Your business is also my business. I helped you to obtain this opera house and I am the one who brings in the paying public. Now see that you get out of my way." Kathleen sidestepped Will and craned her neck to look around him.

Grace and Theodora could clearly hear their raised voices through the open window. Cautiously, they peered inside.

It all happened so suddenly, Grace could not believe her own eyes. When Kathleen moved, Will grabbed her shoulders catching her off balance. He shoved her backwards with a force that threw her over a steamer trunk and she fell heavily. Grace heard the sickening clunk of Kathleen's head against the very same chest of drawers that she had swept sawdust underneath the night before.

"Get up, Kathleen," Will demanded. "I do not need any of your theatrical scenes just now."

Kathleen Carter did not move.

Will stared down at her.

"Kathleen?" he shouted again. He stepped over the trunk and

took her head in his hands. It fell limply back against the chest of drawers. Desperately, he slapped her cheek in an attempt to awaken her, but Kathleen Carter lay motionless on the dirt floor. Her body was contorted in a lifeless pose.

Grace was so close to the windowpane, she saw her breath on the glass. It was coming out in gasps of panic. Suddenly, her foot slipped on the coarse gravel beneath her and her forehead banged against the glass causing the window to shudder in its frame.

Will shot a look in their direction. "Who is there?" he shouted, darting up from the floor and rushing toward the window.

Without delay, Grace and Theodora ran from the alley. When they reached the street, Theodora pointed toward Main Street.

"The sheriff must get involved now," she yelled. "Run to his house as fast as you can, Grace!"

"Theodora, I am so sorry. I lost my footing and I know he saw us."

"Not to worry, Grace. Will McClanahan has gone too far this time. Sheriff Knapp simply cannot deny us now."

Holding their skirts high above their ankles, they raced down Main Street toward City Hall. Grace dared not look behind her for fear that Will McClanahan would be right on her heels.

The white frame house belonging to the sheriff was dark. Theodora took the front steps two at a time and banged on the door. She called loudly for the sheriff. Grace strained to see down Main Street. She imagined Will McClanahan pursuing them, catching up to them and brutally killing them on the spot. What was taking Sheriff Knapp so long?

After what seemed an interminable amount of time, the portly sheriff opened the door a crack and peered out. Seeing Grace and Theodora, he opened the door wide enough for them to enter and lumbered backwards into the foyer, sighing heavily and motioning them inside. He drew the tattered robe he was wearing more tightly around his middle and pulled off his nightcap.

"Ladies, to what do I owe the pleasure of a visit at this late hour?" he said, squinting at them in the darkness and bowing slightly with his nightcap in hand.

"Sheriff Knapp, we have just witnessed a murder," Theodora said bluntly.

"Murder, you say? In Benton Harbor? I do not recall such a thing ever happening here." Sheriff Knapp clucked his tongue as he talked and smoothed his rumpled hair. His mocking tone betrayed his disbelief. Backing into the hallway, he dropped his cap on a shelf and turned up the wick on an oil lamp. He struck a match to light it.

"Sheriff! We need you to come to the Yore Opera House right this instant," Theodora demanded. "We clearly saw Mr. Will McClanahan murder Mrs. Kathleen Carter."

"Will McClanahan again, huh? You ladies surely have it in for that poor man." He crossed his arms over his chest in a defensive gesture. "I think you had better tell me all about it. Shall I prepare some tea?"

"No! He pushed her over a steamer trunk in the basement of the opera house. She hit her head on a chest of drawers and that was it." Theodora's voice was rising in anger at the delay.

"You say she fell over a trunk?" His tone was patronizing.

"I said Will McClanahan pushed her. He shoved her with such a force that she fairly flew over a steamer trunk and struck her head on a chest of drawers. We both saw him do it."

"Where were you when all of this happened?" He looked from Grace to Theodora as if they were the guilty parties.

"We were in the alley observing from a window. We saw all of it quite clearly and we heard them arguing about money."

"You were in the alley at— " he glanced at the clock on a shelf in the hallway, " —midnight? What in heaven's name were you doing there at this hour?"

"We were planning to retrieve something that belongs to Miss Lily Cross."

"At midnight?" He scratched his belly and muttered to himself.

"Yes, sheriff. At midnight. Now will you please come?"

Grace prayed for Theodora to find the strength not to provoke the sheriff into delaying them any further.

"Let me get dressed," he said with resignation. He lumbered down the hallway causing every board to squeak like a tortured symphony tuning up. Grace wondered that the boards did not break under his weight.

110

Sheriff Knapp took his time getting dressed and hitching up his horse to a small carriage. It was after one o'clock when they returned to the opera house. When he jumped to the ground, Grace thought she felt the earth vibrate. He surveyed the grounds with a perfunctory glance that Grace was certain was for their benefit and lumbered up the steps to the side door. It was locked. The front door was also bolted from the inside.

"Looks like we will have to prevail upon Mr. McClanahan to let us in," he said in a voice reserved for women and the feeble minded.

Theodora stared at him in anger. She opened her mouth to speak.

"Breaking the door down would be against the law," he said shrugging his shoulders and turning away from her.

"By now Mr. McClanahan could have dug a grave and held a funeral," Theodora snapped.

He turned back and glared at her. "We have laws, Dr. Goodhart, I enforce the laws."

Theodora bit her lip.

The McClanahan house was dark when the sheriff finally pulled into the yard. Grace and Theodora remained in the carriage while he climbed the steps and knocked on the front door. After several minutes, Will McClanahan opened the door wearing a nightshirt and cap.

"Humpf! He arrives at the door in costume, a nice touch, indeed!" Theodora grumbled to Grace.

"So sorry to bother you at this hour, Mr. McClanahan," the sheriff said cocking his head in the direction of the carriage. "But these ladies say they have witnessed a *murder* in your opera house." He pronounced the word incredibly, as if murder was an inconceivable act for the quiet city of Benton Harbor. "Would you mind terribly coming along with us so I can have a look inside the opera house?"

"At this hour?" McClanahan said scratching his head and pretending to yawn.

"I presume you have been sleeping?" the sheriff asked.

"All night, sir."

The sheriff murmured something that Grace could not hear

111

and Will McClanahan retreated into the house. A short time passed before he came out fully dressed in fresh clothing. He greeted Grace and Theodora cordially as if nothing had ever transpired between them. Theodora gritted her teeth and held tightly to the sides of the carriage. The sheriff chatted amiably with Will as they drove to the opera house.

Inside, Will McClanahan made a show of turning on all of the electric lights. He conducted the walk from the front door to the basement like a tour operator on a steamship, babbling on about the uses of each room as they passed through them. Grace thought he had missed his calling, performances like his belonged on a stage.

It was no surprise to either woman when they entered the basement to find it devoid of Kathleen's body as well as the gargoyles. The dirt floor had been swept clean of sawdust and footprints.

"Is this where you saw the murder?" Sheriff Knapp asked. He made no attempt to keep the mocking tone out of his voice. He smiled indulgently at Will McClanahan who smiled back. Grace felt her indignation rising as the two men played the roles of genteel citizens doing their jobs to placate the interfering local do-gooders.

"Right here," Theodora insisted stepping over to the chest of drawers where Kathleen had banged her head. "She hit her head right on the corner of this chest."

The sheriff blew dust off of the top of the chest. "Appears that this place is largely unused, Mr. McClanahan. Is that so?"

"We store stage properties here when they are not in use. I do not believe I have been down here since the last show closed. Some of the crew might have been though."

"Are you going to conduct a search?" Grace asked.

Sheriff Knapp looked around helplessly at the piles of crates, furniture, costumes and properties that filled the vast expanse of the basement. "Mrs. Shepard, with all due respect for your fine husband and family. I think this can wait until morning. But I assure you that after I investigate Mrs. Carter's, ahem, alleged disappearance, I will bring a deputy here and have a thorough looksee."

Grace resigned herself to the sheriff's disbelief. Any further discussion of their accusations would do no good at this point. Grace wondered where Will had hidden the body. There were at least a dozen likely places within a few feet of where Kathleen had fallen, and probably hundreds of other hiding places within the opera house's many rooms. But the sheriff was leading them to the door and Will McClanahan was turning out the lights behind them. Nothing further was to be accomplished this evening.

The next morning Grace and Theodora were at the sheriff's doorstep just after dawn. Again, he answered the door wearing a robe and nightcap.

"Mrs. Shepard, Dr. Goodhart," he said shaking his head and squinting at the rising sun on the skyline. "Do you ladies ever sleep?"

"Sheriff Knapp, there has been a murder," Theodora said struggling to keep the exasperation out of her voice. "Mr. Will McClanahan has the body of Mrs. Kathleen Carter hidden somewhere inside the Yore Opera House. We do not intend to allow him to dispose of it further."

The sheriff straightened his posture as much as the bulge stretching the middle of his bathrobe allowed him. With his skinny legs and protruding stomach, Grace thought Sheriff Knapp resembled a snake digesting a rat.

When he coughed to clear his throat, Grace fervently hoped he would refrain from spitting. "Ladies, I believe I told you late last evening that I need to investigate whether or not Mrs. Kathleen Carter is missing at all, and— "

Theodora interrupted swiftly. In her most persuasive tone, she said, "May we help? We are dressed and Mrs. Shepard's carriage is at the ready. We could visit the Carter mansion on your behalf and return here with a report for you, sir, before you are finished with your breakfast."

Seeing an interlude from Grace and Theodora's persistent demands, Sheriff Knapp readily accepted their offer. "Now, mind that you do not put words in their mouths," he cautioned as they retreated hastily from his porch. "And remember, ladies, you are not officially deputized."

113

"That was so good of you, Theodora, calling him 'sir'," Grace said when they were in the carriage and on their way.

"That man is such an oaf. I wanted to shake him and scream at him to get him moving; but I knew that would do no good, so I acquiesced. I feel like a hypocrite."

"Sometimes, hypocrisy is the only way to get things done."

❦ Chapter Seventeen

CAUGHT IN THE ACT

The Carter mansion on the southern end of town appeared empty and foreboding at this early hour. The three story home rose on two sides into steeply arched Queen Anne turrets that pierced sharply into the gray sky. Grace wondered if she was letting her imagination run away with her as she turned every shadowy tree and shrub surrounding the property into symbols of Kathleen's death.

Still, the house looked macabre. The untended grounds were overgrown and littered with the debris of neglect. The smell of death hung in the air and Grace could not deny the musty scent of it.

She secured Belle to Carter's hitching post and they climbed from the carriage and approached the front entrance. Slatted, wooden chairs sat in uneven rows on the porch with small stack tables between them. All of the furniture was wet with dew and appeared unwelcoming in the early morning dampness.

Theodora knocked insistently on the elaborately carved wooden door frame and strained to see through the wavy, leaded glass set in its center. Almost immediately, she discerned a brisk movement from within and heard the scraping sound of a bolt being slid away from the door.

Young Emily Carter threw open the door and stood in the threshold. She let her arms drop dejectedly to her sides. Her usually bright face was faded in a puzzled frown which emphasized the dark circles under her eyes and the disarray of her hair. The soft woolen dress she was wearing was wrinkled as though she had slept in it. Grace thought Emily looked more worn and tired than anyone of her youth deserved to be.

"Mrs. Shepard, Dr. Goodhart," she said sadly, "I thought you might be mother."

Grace thought the child might burst into tears.

"Your mother is not at home, then?" Theodora asked knowing full well that only one answer could be made to her question.

"She went to the opera house late last evening and did not return. She finds that necessary from time to time when she is working on a script — there is a daybed in her dressing room, you know — but last night I expected her back so I waited up for her all night. She failed to mention that she was not coming home." Emily looked embarrassed as if the whereabouts of her mother were her responsibility.

"Miss Emily, dear," Grace began speaking in a motherly voice, "will you, please, fetch your wrap and come with us — "

"What's happened to my mother!" Emily exclaimed hearing the concern in Grace's voice. Emily's pink cheeks drained to a frightening shade of gray.

"She has been hurt, Miss Emily. We need you to accompany us to the home of Sheriff Knapp and tell him what you just told us, so he can help."

"But she's all right?" Emily searched the faces of the two women standing before her and waited for an answer. Hearing none, the young girl wailed as tears ran down her cheeks. "Tell me what happened. What has happened to my mother?"

"Miss Emily, allow me to get your wrap," Grace said crossing the threshold to the polished brass hooks in the foyer. She helped the sobbing girl into her light cape and placed a bonnet on her head. Leading her down the steps to the carriage, Grace put her arm around Emily's shoulder and said, "Miss Emily, your mother has been injured. I am sorry, but that is all we are able to say for now. Sheriff Knapp requires your help with his investigation."

"Investigation?" Emily looked up sharply at the word. "Someone hurt her, then? It was Mr. McClanahan, I know it. He has hurt her before, mother always says that is the way it is between men and women."

"That is the way it was between *them*, Miss Emily," Theodora interjected. "That is not the way for most men and women."

"He always came back with presents," Emily said. "And that made everything all right again between him and mother."

Grace could not find the words to say that, this time, he

116

would not be coming back to her mother. She resolved to take the orphan girl home to Helen, Dan and the children after she told her story to the sheriff.

Sheriff Knapp listened attentively as Emily Carter related the events of last evening and this morning. Now, he could not deny the fact that Kathleen Carter had left for the opera house late last night — just as Grace and Theodora had reported — and had not returned to her home. Finally, the sheriff would have to make a thorough search of the opera house. Grace hoped he would do it immediately, before Will McClanahan had further opportunity to dispose of Kathleen's body.

They left City Hall and drove east on Main Street, turning north on Sixth to Territorial Road. Grace intended to tell Emily the truth about her mother as soon as she had the girl settled into Helen's warm kitchen; she pondered the words she might use as the carriage clattered over the bumpy road.

Neither Theodora nor Emily said a word as they traveled past the opera house at the corner of Sixth and Territorial. Its imposing four-story presence threw a shadow into the alleyway west of the rising sun where Grace caught a glimpse of two men hauling a steamer trunk onto the back of a wagon.

"Miss Emily," Grace said urgently. "I need thread and cloth for a new pillow. Your needlepoint skills are so advanced, would you select the materials for me?"

Grace yanked the reins and forced Belle into a sudden turn back toward Main Street. The surprised horse looked alertly at her mistress.

"Is now the proper time to begin a sewing project, Grace?" Theodora said.

"Oh yes, it is absolutely Theodora," Grace said firmly. She whipped Belle into a trot and careened around the corner onto Main Street. Pulling to an abrupt halt in front of Rutledge's General Store, Grace said, "We will pick you up in half an hour, Miss Emily, now hop down quickly please."

The confused girl did as she was told. When Grace pulled away from the store, Theodora demanded, "What was that all about?"

"Look!" Grace pointed in the direction of Sixth Street where

117

Will McClanahan was turning west onto Main Street. He was driving a wagon belonging to the opera house. In its bed was a steamer trunk.

"Do you think?" Theodora uttered.

"I saw him and another man in the alley loading the trunk onto the wagon as we passed by. They did not notice us."

"What better place to hide a body — especially one as diminutive as Kathleen's — than in a padlocked steamer trunk."

Will McClanahan drove the wagon brazenly past City Hall and Sheriff Knapp's office. Some traffic was out on the street and downtown merchants were opening their doors for the day's business. Grace followed at a distance keeping her eyes on Will McClanahan's back. He turned the wagon into the entrance to the docks at the far end of the ship canal. At this point in the season, commercial shipping had not yet reached its harvesttime peak. Grace prayed that someone would be at the docks to help them.

Turning the corner, Grace heard a splash. She guided Belle into the broad entrance in time to see Will McClanahan climbing into his wagon which was perched perilously close to the edge of the vast platform extending out over the ship canal. Behind him, the wagon's bed was empty.

Will McClanahan stared at Theodora and Grace. His expression was drawn into a tight line punctuated with piercing eyes that immediately understood. He was caught. They would only have to retrieve the trunk from the deep waters of the shipping canal to prove his guilt. He pulled a gun from his coat pocket and pointed it toward Grace and Theodora.

"Stop it now, Will McClanahan!" Theodora shouted.

He fired the gun in their direction and the noise from the blast startled his horse who reared up in fright. The wagon's rear wheels rolled backwards, sliding toward the edge of the wooden dock. Will McClanahan grabbed the reins and whipped his horse forward. The horse slid backward as momentum from the wagon's weight pulled the rig closer to the edge.

Grace and Theodora watched in horror as Will McClanahan's screams urged the horse forward. The struggling horse regained its footing and lurched ahead pulling the rear wheels out of danger. Grace breathed a sigh of relief. She tightened her grip on

Belle's reins.

Will McClanahan whipped his horse toward Grace and Theodora. His rig clattered over the gravel. Will raised his gun and pointed it directly at Grace. She saw the gun's barrel less than twenty feet from her face and squeezed her eyes shut.

A deafening blast caused Grace to open her eyes in time to see Will McClanahan's horse slip to its knees. As fast as the horse tumbled, it was up again and running from a fear generated by the second shot from Will's gun. The horse was headed home as fast as the slippery gravel would allow it to run. Will cursed and tried again to focus the gun in Grace's direction, but the jarring movements of the wagon on the gravel made steadying a shot impossible.

Grace seized the opportunity to move her wagon ahead in the opposite direction. Belle obliged by making a path parallel to the ship canal.

"Keep going, Grace!" Theodora shouted. "There is a clearing up ahead where we can turn back to the main road."

"I know the place."

Theodora turned around on the seat. "He is not following us."

"He has a gun, Grace."

"So do I."

"What?"

"I am sorry, Theo, but I felt the need for it after what transpired at the opera house between Will McClanahan and Evan Howell. I arranged for it then."

"Could you use it?"

Grace turned to Theodora. She stared hard into her eyes. "Yes, Theo. I could use it if I had to. Will McClanahan has no remorse. I saw that in his aura. He beat Kathleen. He drugged Miss Lily repeatedly and embezzled the opera house from her. He fought viciously with Evan Howell. We have no idea what he has done to his own family. All we know for certain is that Will McClanahan is capable of anything."

"Then let's go to Sheriff Knapp and get him to arrest Will McClanahan."

"Upon what evidence? Kathleen's body is lying on the bottom of the shipping canal."

"Sheriff Knapp can bring it up."

"Allowing Will McClanahan to escape with Miss Lily's gold in the meantime? Not on your life, Theodora. Will McClanahan is headed straight for the opera house at this moment. I would bet on it. He is after that gold and I intend to prevent him from stealing any more from Miss Lily. We are here to help her, Theo. We need to do this and we need to do it now."

❦ Chapter Eighteen

TRAGEDY AT THE YORE OPERA HOUSE

Grace gripped the reins and urged Belle forward with a firm flick of her wrists. Theodora saw the determination in her small hands. She did not need to look at Grace's face to know that this was the end.

As they passed the point near the banks of the shipping canal where they had arrived some nine months ago, Theodora visualized the time slip. It had presented itself to Cynthia and she had been able to bring Karla with her from the present to the past.

A slip in time. For Cynthia it had been a passage of strong desire. It was as if she had willed the delicate time slip to be there for them with its wavy oval edges and its warm entrance enveloping them into the past as they passed through it. Cynthia had selected four smooth stones from the canal bank and stood quietly holding two of the thick stones in each of her open palms. She had recited a soft chant to acknowledge the spiritual world surrounding them.

Karla had accepted her hand and together they had slipped through the wavy edges of the passageway and drifted into the time slip's ethereal smoothness. It had immediately embraced them with protection.

Theodora prayed for that protection now.

"We will have the protection you are praying for Theo," Grace said without turning to look at her friend. Her eyes were fixed on the path just ahead of Belle.

The packed sand and gravel on the banks of the canal was rutted and bumpy. She steered Belle gently around the deepest potholes.

Theodora looked at Grace and saw the force of her entire

121

being reflected in her expression. It was clear that Grace had become stronger since Karla Cifelli had entered her life. The purpose they shared had given them direction throughout this slip in time. Now it was time to conclude their journey.

Grace pulled back on the left rein and Belle turned the carriage onto Main Street. Theodora straightened her coat. The paving bricks on Benton Harbor's main street afforded a much smoother ride than the gravel along the banks of the ship canal.

Grace urged Belle into a brisk trot.

"Hang on, Theodora. He has a good start on us."

"Perhaps the interval will give him the illusion of time."

"He will think that we are not coming after him. That we are too afraid."

The idea gave Theodora a new courage. She said, "If we enter the opera house stealthily, we will be able to catch him off guard."

"I will leave Belle and the carriage near the Thayer Company's office."

"She will be secure there."

Grace brought the carriage to a halt near Thayer's hitching post. She wrapped the reins in a double knot and patted Belle's neck. After the brisk trot down Main Street, the horse felt warm to the touch. Grace went back to the carriage and pulled a blanket from under the seat. She tossed it over Belle's back and straightened the sides.

Theodora had already walked to the corner of the building and was peering inside. The fruit packaging office was empty. At this time of the year, everyone would be working in the warehouse.

Grace caught up with Theodora. They walked quickly along the side of the Thayer building, past Schuder & Stein's saloon and Joseph Frick's building. As they approached the front of the opera house, they saw McClanahan's horse and carriage.

Theodora stopped. "Look Grace, the door is ajar. Do you suppose he is waiting for us?"

"No. I think he left it open in his haste for the gold. He is a greedy man, Theo. He is also arrogant. I feel certain that he thinks he is quite alone at least for the time being. He knows how slowly

Sheriff Knapp reacts to us."

They walked quietly past the ticket office to the auditorium door. It stood wide open to the blackness beyond it. Grace stopped at the entrance and listened. She held her breath. She strained for the slightest sound, but heard nothing.

"He has gone below," she whispered to Theodora.

They proceeded down the thickly carpeted left aisle to the steps at the side of the stage. Crossing quickly through the backstage area, they reached the door that led to the dressing rooms. It too was open.

The open spaces of the opera house were connected by aisles and corridors. Most of the doors to dressing rooms and offices were closed.

Grace began to walk more slowly as they approached the basement door. She did not allow her heels to touch the floor as she pulled the wooden door open. She held her breath again. Mercifully, the door did not creak.

Grace let her breath escape as she moved to the landing just inside the door. Theodora stood close behind her.

They could see the light on the far side of the basement. He must have moved the gargoyles to the north side of the room, Grace thought. McClanahan was out of sight, but Grace and Theodora could hear the rasping sound of a hand saw drawn across thick wood.

They tiptoed down the stairs careful to place their feet near the wall where the risers would be less likely to creak under their weight. Theodora followed Grace as they took the steps one at a time.

McClanahan's back was to them. He was bent over with his left foot holding one of the gargoyles in place. They could see the rhythmic rise and fall of his elbow over a handsaw.

Grace and Theodora stood still at the bottom of the stairs. Grace extracted the gun from her purse. Her face was set in an expression of fearless determination. She moved into the room and Theodora followed her.

"Will McClanahan!" Grace shouted when they reached the center of the basement. "Stop what you are doing and put your hands on your head!"

123

McClanahan's arm abruptly ceased sawing and he turned toward the women standing in the middle of the room. Without hesitation, he yanked the saw from the gargoyle and attempted to fling it at Grace and Theodora. But the blade caught in the cut and caused his aim to falter. The handsaw flew through the air toward the ceiling in front of them and ripped into the electrical wiring hanging from the rafters. Sparks ignited Theodora's skirts as the blade tore through the snarl of wiring.

McClanahan lunged after the saw. He grabbed it as it hung from the thick black cords and pulled it toward him. The metal blade slicing through the live wires sent an electrical shock down the saw that jolted McClanahan off of his feet. He seemed unable to release the handle of the saw until the force of the electricity sent him to his knees. The saw clattered to the floor beside him. As he fell, he grasped the wrist of his right hand. The palm of his hand had turned black where it had gripped the saw handle.

"Were it not for the wood of that handle, you would be dead Mr. McClanahan," Theodora said evenly.

Grace dropped her gun into the purse hanging from her arm. She grabbed a broom and began to methodically beat at the smoldering folds of Theodora's skirts.

"The sparks appear to be out. Thank you, Grace," Theodora said looking down at the singed material in the front of her skirts.

When she looked back at Will McClanahan he was holding his gun in his good hand. The barrel was pointing straight at Grace.

"Place your gun on the floor, Mrs. Shepard," he said, rising from his knees with a visible effort.

Grace stared hard at him. His face winced with the pain of his burned hand as he used it to support the weight of the gun in his left.

"That's it. Nice and easy. Put the gun on the floor," he said as she extracted her gun from the drawstring bag and bent to the dirt floor. "Now, pick up the saw and finish the job I started before you meddling ladies interrupted me."

Theodora held the gargoyle steady while Grace sawed through the wood of its neck. McClanahan had barely begun on this one and there was one more gargoyle left to open. Grace sawed until her shoulders ached. The task seemed more difficult with the barrel of Will McClanahan's gun forcing the work. Finally, the last of the gold spilled to the floor.

"There are canvas bags in that trunk. Open it," McClanahan ordered. He had moved to a chair and sat down heavily.

"Mr. McClanahan, it would be wise for me to look at your hand. My bag is in the carriage. I could bandage it for you," Theodora offered.

He glared at her. "Fill the bags with the coins and move them to the window."

Theodora glared back at him and picked an empty canvas bag from the steamer trunk. She noticed that the trunk's bottom held several full bags. He had hidden the coins from the first gargoyle inside the trunk.

When all of the coins were bagged, Grace and Theodora carried them to the window.

"Now sit on the floor. You there, Mrs. Shepard. Doctor, you sit over here."

"Whatever for?" Theodora asked.

"Because we cannot move the gold until dark. Since you ladies arrived here so promptly, it is safe to assume that you did not stop to inform Sheriff Knapp. Now sit."

Grace moved to a chair near the trunk and sat down.

"Not there, Mrs. Shepard. On the floor. You, too, Dr. Goodhart. Take a place on the floor. Over there."

Grace sat down on the dirt floor. She adjusted the long folds of her skirts underneath her and looked at Theodora. She was leaning against a brick wall on the far side of the basement.

Without light from the bulb the basement was lit only from dim daylight from the small windows near the top of one basement wall. Since the windows opened onto the alley, very little traffic crossed through. The basement smelled acrid with the residue from the electrical sparking and the room was filled with smokey shadows. But Grace could clearly see the barrel of Will McClanahan's gun pointing straight at her. He did not seem to mind the pain of his burned hand.

"Now, tell me where the rest of my gold is hidden."

Grace stared at him.

125

"Mrs. Shepard. The whereabouts of my gold?"

"I have no idea what you are asking about."

"I think you do, but no matter, we will collect it when we leave here. And you will tell me, Mrs. Shepard, or I will shoot Dr. Goodhart before your very eyes."

"I think you intend to kill us both anyway. It would seem that I have nothing to lose by keeping silent."

He moved toward her with his hand raised as if to strike her. She raised her chin in defiance and closed her eyes.

But the blow did not come. When Grace opened her eyes, she saw Will McClanahan rubbing the wrist muscles of his burned hand. The effort of carrying the gun and raising his fist to hit her had caused him too much pain. He slumped back into his chair and nursed his aching hand.

Hours passed slowly. Grace leaned her head against the curve of the lid of a steamer trunk and fell asleep. When she awoke her legs felt stiff from the cold of the basement floor.

Will McClanahan was standing at the bottom of the stairs with his head cocked to one side as if he was listening intently to something up above. Grace glanced at Theodora. She was leaning against the bricks with her head tilted to her shoulder in sleep.

Grace thought she heard voices from above. She sat quietly and listened. There were voices! Someone had come to rescue them!

Will McClanahan strode across the room with his gun held evenly in front of him.

In a low voice, he said, "If you make one sound, I will shoot you both. I have nothing to lose and believe me I will see you dead before I am caught."

"Give up, Mr. McClanahan. They have come to rescue us and it will be easier on you if you cooperate with the authorities."

Theodora shifted on the floor. She roused herself and turned in their direction. "What is it?" she asked.

"People are upstairs, Theo," Grace said. "It will only be a matter of time before they find us down here."

"They have no reason to come down here. This basement is used for storage and little else. They are here for a benefit performance," McClanahan said in a whisper. "If you ladies make so

126

much as a whimper, I promise you I will shoot you both without a moment's hesitation. Now stay quiet."

"Someone will come down here, Mr. McClanahan and we will be here. It will be so much better for you if you let us go."

"And have you tell them that Kathleen's body is lying on the bottom of the ship canal? That I have discovered hidden gold coins in the building I manipulated away from Miss Lily? I do not think so. Better that I take my chances with you until the show is over. Then we will carry the bags to my carriage, collect the coins you have stolen from me, and I will be long gone from Benton Harbor by morning."

Grace could still see the barrel of Will McClanahan's gun in the dusky light. Above it, his face was grim with hatred. If he felt fear, it did not show. She knew he was right, he had nothing to lose. He would surely kill them on the spot at the slightest provocation. She leaned back against the trunk and waited.

The noise from above increased as the opera house filled with people. The shuffling of feet on the auditorium floor could be discerned. It must be nearly eight o'clock in the evening, the time when opera house performances usually began.

Dan would be frantic with worry. He would be out searching for her by now. Would he think to look for her here? She had left Belle and the carriage at the Thayer Company. They could have gone in any direction from there.

Grace laid her head on the curve of the trunk and sighed.

The noise from above was muffled. She could hear strains from a piano, but could not make out the tune. The performance was going on. Grace doubted if anyone would hear her scream even if she dared to do it. Will McClanahan had nothing to lose. He most certainly would shoot them at once.

The acrid smell in the basement seemed worse than before. It burned her eyes. Ventilation in the room was minimal, but some of the electrical smell should have dissipated by now, Grace thought. Instead, it seemed to increase. Was there smoke in the room? Grace could not tell. The basement was completely dark except for a small amount of moonlight coming in through the windows.

Soon, a thunder of applause could be heard. Then another

127

song. Grace squirmed on the floor. Her right leg had fallen asleep. She shook it out.

"Be still," McClanahan snarled.

"I think the wiring is smoking where you cut through it with the saw," Theodora whispered.

"Shut up!"

"Mr. McClanahan, it is getting difficult to breath down here. We need get out of here before we suffocate from smoke inhalation."

"We will be out soon enough," he whispered harshly. "Until then, just stay where you are."

He turned the gun on Theodora and sat heavily on a chair. More applause filled the hall above them. Then the scraping and shuffling of feet on the wooden auditorium floor. The performance was over. People were leaving.

Half an hour passed and there was no sound from above. Will McClanahan moved again to the stairway and listened.

"All clear," he said, walking back to where they were sitting. "Get up. It's time to load my carriage."

Suddenly sparks shot down from the tangle of wiring and ignited the flimsy stage properties and the worn costumes below the rafters. The rafters themselves burst into flames and rose to the floorboards above. The basement was filled with light from the quick burst of fire. The smoldering wires had finally caught on the dried wood and the fire spread instantaneously.

"Grace, to the stairway!" Theodora shouted.

Grace started to get up and both women moved toward the exit.

"Hold it right there!" Will McClanahan held his gun in his good hand. The barrel was pointed directly at Grace. "Mrs. Shepard, get to the window and push the coins outside. You, too, doctor!"

Grace tried to think where she had dropped her gun. Through the smoke, she could not distinguish the form of a gun anywhere on the floor.

"Over by the windows, both of you!" McClanahan shouted. He motioned toward the canvas bags. Move them outside. Now!"

"Mr. McClanahan, please. We do not have time. Let us help

128

you out of here before the entire place goes up in flames."

He stumbled toward them through the smoke. Grace saw the gun held steadily in his left hand. "You are not leaving here. Now move!"

Grace and Theodora moved cautiously around the flaming rafters toward the basement windows. Will McClanahan followed them closely through the thickening smoke. A table caught fire beneath the rafters. It would only be seconds before more of the stage properties would catch. The floorboards were burned through and flames shot upward toward the backstage area above. Theodora hurried to the window. Her eyes watered as she strained to locate a bag of gold.

"You, too, Mrs. Shepard," McClanahan ordered.

Theodora straightened up as Grace bent behind her and fished into the pile for another bag. Theodora passed between Grace and Will McClanahan and hurried toward the window. She pushed one canvas bag through to the alley and then another. She coughed and could not catch her breath. In a minute they would all be overcome by the thick smoke.

When a rafter crashed to the floor with a deafening roar, it took Theodora a moment to look back. Grace turned beside her and squinted into the smokey room.

Will McClanahan was lying on his back under the rafter. A pool of blood formed an uneven circle around him. The heavy rafter had severed his arm. The gun was still clutched in the hand that now lay apart from his body. Another heavy rafter crashed to the floor obscuring Will McClanahan from view. Flames shot through the ceiling with a force of heat that knocked Theodora against the wall.

She pulled the window down with a strength she did not know existed and helped Grace through the tiny opening. Grace leaned back inside and pulled Theodora into the alley.

In the fresh air, Theodora coughed the smoke out of her lungs and turned to Grace. "We must sound the fire alarm!"

They ran down Sixth Street and onto Main Street toward City Hall. With the alarm given, Grace and Theodora ran back to the opera house. As Grace and Theodora watched the blaze, they heard the sound of locomotives and other whistles and bells sounding the news of the fire throughout the city.

It was nearing midnight. A crowd was gathering as the hose carts rattled to a halt around the opera house. Firemen from Benton Harbor and St. Joseph responded to the call. Many lines of hose were hooked up to the fire hydrants in the vicinity of Sixth and Territorial Streets. The men poured water onto the blazing building which had become an inferno of flames fanned by the night wind.

Hundreds of spectators looked on as the men positioned ladders along the brick wall in the alley. Without warning, the top part of the wall on the alley side of the building gave in and crushed the men who stood there. Tons of debris came crashing down with a roar that enveloped the alley in an avalanche of falling bricks and flames. Smoke poured from the structure.

Theodora attempted to enter the alley to assist the men who had been working there. She was pushed back by the heat. Portions of bodies could be seen through the smoke and the fallen wall. Grace estimated that at least twenty men were buried in the ruins. She rushed to Theodora's side and pulled her back.

"It is too dangerous, Theo. The heat is too intense."

At that moment, Grace saw a fireman turn his hose on Mr. Bernstein who was attempting to enter his clothing store at the rear of the building. He and his clerk were screaming. Everything they owned was being consumed by the fire.

Dr. Bostick saw them then and yelled to Theodora. He stood and motioned for her to assist him with a gray haired man who had burned his hands trying to remove bricks that had fallen on the firemen.

Sparks flew in all directions. The buildings adjoining the opera house were doused with water to stop the fire from spreading.

Grace worked steadily with Theodora as she assisted the injured firemen and bystanders who attempted to quell the flames. The opera house burned into the wee hours of the morning and on into the next day. By daylight, they were all exhausted. By Grace's count, at least twelve men had already died and several more were critically injured.

When the wounded were finally all accounted for and the fire was under control, Grace and Theodora walked slowly back to the Thayer Company.

They found Belle still tied to the post outside the office. The horse's eyes were glazed with terror at the smell of the smoke and the noise of the firemen. Grace calmed her and led her away from the disaster. When they turned onto Main Street, Grace and Theodora boarded the carriage. Grace flicked the reins and turned the rig toward Theodora's office.

"I must let Dan know that I am safe. Will you come with me?"

"I cannot. I need to get a few supplies in order to help Dr. Bell and Dr. Bostick with the survivors. Several of those men are badly injured. Their families will be in shock. Come back as soon as you are able. You will find me in one of their homes."

Grace waited while Theodora gathered the necessary medical supplies. She drove Theodora to the home of John Holmes who had been injured trying to save some of his barber equipment. Grace had heard that his business was a total loss.

Sadly, Grace turned Belle in the direction of her home. So much had happened, she could not comprehend how she could begin to explain it all to Dan.

❦ Chapter Nineteen

COMPLETING THE CYCLE

Throughout the autumn months, under Grace's careful supervision, a revolving group of women moved in and out of Miss Lily's abundant house — with more moving out than in. True to form, Miss Lily proved to be a highly volatile charge, especially at first. But as the drugs washed out of her system, replaced by good food and a routine of rest and recreation, she regained the composure of the caring woman she had been before her father died.

By November, two of the women, the Chesley sisters — persuaded initially by generous pay provided from the recovered gold — had become loyal and constant companions providing Miss Lily with friendship as well as care. Now, Grace felt the arrangement might proceed one step further. She approached all three of the women with the idea of the Cross house becoming a permanent home for the sisters as well as for Miss Lily. Grace assured Miss Lily that the house would remain in her name and would entirely belong to her. But would it not be far more convenient especially as winter approached, Grace suggested, if the sisters simply lived in instead of coming and going everyday? They all agreed it would.

A trust fund was operating smoothly under the auspices of the Farmers and Merchants Bank which oversaw the daily management of the Cross family home as well as the needs of the McClanahan family and Miss Emily Carter with whom Miss Lily had decided to share her fortune.

As autumn turned into winter, the number of wagons which rolled past the Shepard house on Territorial Road heading toward the great shipping canal lessened. Grace was fond of watching as teams of horses hauled loads of harvest time produce, lumber and grain to the steamers destined for ports across the waters of Lake

Michigan. She would miss the activity of their frequent passing.

Grace and Helen had finished the necessary autumn cleaning, removing the summer slip covers and rearranging the furniture for the winter months ahead. The woven rugs had been aired and the summer dresses were put away for the season. With the children in school, Grace had the day to herself. She pondered the prospect of working in the garden. A few pumpkins and squash still remained outside. Maybe she should just take a walk? Theodora had said that walking was good for the spine.

Considering her options for the open day ahead of her, Grace walked to the porch to observe the long parade of farm wagons that traveled Territorial Road to the canal. It was the shipping canal that had allowed for Benton Harbor's initial expansion. Constructed in the early 1860s, the canal ran parallel to Main Street. Grace knew that most of the early entrepreneurs had settled their businesses on the canal or near enough to it to take advantage of the access it provided to busy and profitable transportation routes.

Steam ships ferrying passengers to and from Chicago carried as many as two thousand visitors per trip to Benton Harbor during the tourist season. Two of Helen's cousins were arriving late this afternoon. They came every year to relax and refresh; and they told their friends about the rural community on the other side of the lake. People came in droves to escape the dust and the heat of the metropolitan areas where they lived and worked. They left their cares and worries on the Chicago docks when they embarked on the journey across Lake Michigan en route to Benton Harbor and St. Joseph.

Grace walked around the large house and proceeded slowly to the well just outside the kitchen door. She drew up a bucket full of the sweet-tasting spring water. She no longer had to carry pails of water from the well — Dan had recently buried pipes from the spring to a pump in the kitchen — but on long days like this one Grace still indulged in dropping the wooden bucket deep into the cool well and listening to the echo of rippling water as it plunked into the depths. There would not be many more mild days like this one. Grace could feel the chill of winter in the air.

The back yard of the rambling white farm house was edged

with apricot trees. Planted in neat rows by Dan's grandfather, the apricot orchards blended into more than one hundred acres of peach trees. Now, all of the trees were bare of the fruit they had harvested and shipped in recent months. Grace and Helen had spent many hours canning the peaches and apricots and cooking them down into sweet jams and jellies. It had been a good year. They would eat well this winter.

The Shepard farm, along with other early farms, had given Benton Harbor a reputation for producing fruit that was as tasty as any in the world. Grace walked to the edge of the yard where the fragrance of the apricot trees still pervaded the air with a sweet perfume. The smell was not as strong as it was in the spring when the lovely blossoms seemed to fill the town with their scent, but it was there and Grace filled her lungs with its goodness.

"Grace," Helen called from the kitchen window. "You have a visitor."

"Thank you, Helen," Grace called back, "Who is it?"

"Dr. Goodhart."

Theodora was waiting on the wide porch which circled the big white house on the hill when Grace walked around to the front yard. The porch was arranged with cushioned wooden furniture which would have to be taken in soon. Helen's pots of geraniums still stood in their places at either side of the steps. They would be hung in the root cellar to lie dormant all winter, until next year when they would blossom and grow again.

"Theodora, what a nice surprise," Grace said. "Helen told me you were here."

When she had settled into a rocker, Theodora looked intently at Grace. Her clear, blue eyes shone like polished disks of moonstone and Grace knew instinctively what news was forthcoming.

"It is time for us to slip back into the future," Theodora said without preamble.

"Oh," Grace said letting her breath flow on the word. She leaned back in the generous rocking chair and the wood creaked in several places along the slats. "I have become so comfortable here. Life is so slow now, so easy."

"I know, Grace. I know," Theodora let her words flow out

slowly. She watched as a flat wagon loaded with pumpkins passed in front of the Shepard's sloping yard. "But we have accomplished what we were called to do. It is time to go forward from here."

"What will happen to the children, to Dan and Helen, without me?" Grace sat up in alarm at the thought.

"Grace will still be here," Theodora said gently. "She will be a little wiser, perhaps a bit more progressive for having shared a part of Karla Cifelli, but she will remain here in 1896. Just as Karla and Cynthia are waiting at the ship canal in the future."

"When do we leave?"

"We can go anytime before midnight on the winter solstice."

"That is next month." Grace rocked back in the chair and closed her eyes. The rhythmic creaks of the wooden rocking chair reminded her of the many long nights when she had rocked Susan to sleep, slowly, patiently, humming softly to the strains of the chair's consistent comforting creaking. A warm tear slid out of the corner of her eye and ran down one smooth cheek.

"I wanted to give you time to make your farewells and to arrange that particular evening away from home. We can perform the ritual at my house and walk to the canal from there."

PART THREE:
AND BACK AGAIN

AND BACK AGAIN

In a surround of warm mist
The clean damp smell enclosed them.
Their minds impressed with a sense
Of it all, present and past.

In their journey, they became
Closer to all parts of the Earth,
Every person, Every season,
Every place and all directions.

Cynthia Marigold

❦ **Chapter Twenty**

THE RITUAL OF PASSAGE

On a mild night in early December, Grace tied Belle snugly to the hitching post at Theodora's front entrance. She pulled a carrot from her handbag and fed it to Belle. The horse nuzzled her shoulder and Grace patted the animal's neck. Karla would miss the loyal horse and the pleasant times she had enjoyed in the open air of the carriage. Now, she was returning to the modern confines of cars and closed buildings. Karla resolved to ease herself into a slower, more deliberate lifestyle.

The influence of Grace Shepard upon Karla Cifelli would insure that Karla remembered the pleasant carriage rides, the long walks, the perfumed scent of the orchards and the smell of wet earth after a rain. Karla would not forget the simple pleasures of flower pots on porches and horses in the fields.

Inside, Theodora had her kitchen prepared for the ritual of passage back to the future. A large bowl of water was centered on her circular table. Squash leaves and late daisies from her garden and shells from Lake Michigan were arranged around the bowl. Theodora cast the circle with a willow stick and invoked the directions of north, south, east and west. She thanked each direction for assistance and guidance and lit a single red candle next to the water bowl. Grace lit her candle and both women purified their hands in the water before selecting a fresh leaf to wash away their worries.

Grace picked the stem from a daisy and floated the blossom in the bowl. She thought of Emily Carter and prayed for her protection and well-being.

Theodora floated a yellow daisy for Lily Cross and another one for their safe passage through the slip. As Theodora chanted softly, Grace felt her worries float away and dissolve in the quiet peace of the cleansing ritual. With a lighter heart, she let a flower go for Dan. She floated another one for Helen and one for each of her children.

Finally, Grace picked a blossom for her loyal horse, Belle, and let it free upon the water. She prayed for good health and protection for all of them and felt Karla's desire to remain in the past lift away and drift on a gentle current of air into the night. They would all be well. Karla Cifelli and Cynthia Marigold had served their purpose here.

Theodora sang a simple song about completion that made Grace laugh. Theodora was at her best when improvising and tonight was no exception. They had accomplished the assistance they had been called to give. Both women felt warm and fulfilled as they danced slowly, contentedly around the table and reached down to the wooden floor. They pressed their palms to the floorboards, releasing the excess energy they had created between themselves.

The night air was cold as they walked along Main Street toward the docks of the great shipping canal fed by the St. Joseph and the Paw Paw Rivers. The rivers joined together and emptied into the eastern waters of Lake Michigan. Immense rope bound the huge pilings that supported heavy wharf planks along the banks. During daylight hours, the sounds of industry carried across the water as lumber and late produce were shipped away. Now, as the hour of midnight approached, muted echoes of night noises bounced off of the deserted docks. Grace breathed deeply of the moonlit air and wondered if she would ever again breath air as clean and fresh as this.

"Here it is . . ." Theodora said, casting the remains of the ritual into the canal. As the flower stems floated on the current and the candle pieces sank, Grace turned and saw the time slip. Theodora stood in front of it. Its curly edges wafted gently in the wind.

"Are you ready?"

"I suppose I am," Grace replied. She felt a surge of exhilaration and fear mixed with a distant longing to hang back and remain in the past. But she understood that their mission here was completed and the rest of their lives waited on the other side. She stepped nearer to Theodora and glimpsed the creamy brown passage inside of the slip.

"Yes," she amended softly. "I am ready to return."

Theodora selected four smooth stones from the river bank and held two of them in each of her open palms. She recited a simple chant of safe passage and reached out to Grace. Pressing two of the stones into Grace's palm, Theodora covered the hand of her friend with her own and they walked through the shimmering passageway to the future.

Once again, the slip's creamy smoothness enveloped them within its warm mist. Its clean damp smell impressed their minds with a vague sense of everything past and present. In their journey, they had become closer to all parts of the universe, to every season, every person, every place and all directions.

❦ Chapter Twenty-One

THE OTHER SIDE

On the other side the mid-morning sun was shining brightly. Karla felt a shiver of energy running through her body tingling down to the tips of her fingers and toes. She surveyed Cynthia with a broad smile. Gone were the long linen dress and high buttoned shoes she had been wearing in the past. Theodora was back in the blackness of midnight in 1896.

Standing beside Karla, Cynthia looked so pleased with herself, Karla thought she might burst with happiness. Cynthia's shaggy blonde hair bristled with electricity and the three pierced earrings in her right ear glimmered in the bright sunlight. She held two of the stones in her left hand and Karla held the other two where Theodora had pressed them into her palm. All four stones now contained worn holes in their centers as if something gradual and persistent, like the lapping of waves on the shoreline, had passed through their hard surfaces.

Karla looked back just in time to see the indistinct edges of the slip fold in on themselves and disappear. Nothing remained save the banks of the dilapidated canal and the debris that surrounded it.

"Is it gone forever?" Karla asked.

"It will come back the next time it is needed . . ." Cynthia said. "But for now . . . don't you have to open the store?"

"That I do," Karla said, consulting the watch strapped to her wrist: 9:23 a.m. If one only considered the clock, a matter of a few minutes had passed. It was as if they had not been gone at all. But the moments had contained a lifetime.

When they sank into the cushioned seats of Cynthia's car, Karla recalled the comfortable roll of the creaky, wooden rocker on the wide porch of Shepard's rambling house on the hill. She resolved to find an antique rocker for her apartment, but she quickly decided that she could live without the babies that might go with it. After all, she had raised seven children in the past. Her motherly instincts had been fulfilled.

Doily was waiting for her inside the store as Karla unlocked the front door. The bell jangled overhead. Karla dropped her keys into her pocket and stooped over to pick up the black and white cat. Doily stretched her neck toward Karla's face and fixed her large green eyes on Karla's blue ones. The cat purred contentedly, but kept her eyes leveled on Karla's with intense amazement as if she knew that her owner had accomplished something strange and wonderful and new.

The doorbell jangled again and a customer bundled up against the winter chill entered the bookstore. Karla smiled, and said, "Hello, let me know how I can help." She paused just long enough to make the customer feel welcomed, and walked to the back of the store. She pressed the play button on her cassette recorder and savored the sound of the Boston Pops playing "O Holy Night." The song was as familiar today as it had been in the Christmas of 1895.

Karla thought of Grace Shepard's children — her children — singing the same carols, "Silent Night," "Greensleeves," "The First Noel," in the horse-drawn carriage as the Shepard family drove over snowy roads on their way to the old Benton Harbor Methodist church. Karla smiled, savoring her memories until the telephone rang and the front doorbell jangled once more, gently jarring her back into the present. Some things — like the rush before Christmas and the singing of carols — never change, Karla thought. But as for me . . . as for me, I am stronger now. I have taken the risk of reaching out to strengthen others and in the process I am the one who grew.

Doily snuggled into Karla's arms and purred. Karla felt the cat's warm vibrations through her sweater; she took Doily back to the cash register and placed her gently on the countertop. There were customers waiting in line.

It was after nine when Karla finally walked up the stairs to her apartment over the bookstore. It had been a long day. She had not taken time for lunch and she felt hungry and tired. But the soreness in her shoulders felt good, like the ache of muscles after a workout.

❦ Chapter Twenty-Two

A RECORD OF THE PAST

January was traditionally a slow month for retail. Maggie took the month off and Karla used the time to clean and rearrange the store. For Karla, rearranging bookshelves was a slow and consuming endeavor; she had a tendency to linger over titles, scan pages and make personal piles for her own reading.

In the used book stacks, Karla always made a point of ruffling through the pages looking for old bookmarks or historic scraps of paper — checking for money, she said when one customer asked what she was doing.

She thumbed through a copy of *An Early History of Benton Harbor*, and very nearly dropped the book when a yellowed copy of the *Benton Harbor Saturday Herald* slipped out of one of the pages. It was dated September 12, 1896.

The headlines read, "Holocaust in Benton Harbor. Yore Opera House Block Burned to the Ground. Twelve Men Dead. Half a Dozen Others Injured — Some Severely. An Awful Night. Sickening Scenes of Horror — Sad Ruin of a Stately Structure. Loss $52,900. Joseph Frick's Shoe Store and Residence, The Evening News Plant, Bernstein's Clothing Stock, Austin's Bakery and Holmes' Barber Shop Destroyed."

Karla began reading the story of the conflagration and the tragic loss of life as if it had happened only yesterday:

"An awful calamity has visited Benton Harbor — the destruction by fire of the Yore Opera House and the loss of twelve human lives. The city was thrown into a state of excitement recalling the graphic scenes following the loss of the steamer *Chicora* in January, 1895. Many homes are in mourning and half a dozen families are left fatherless by the loss of brave men killed by falling, blazing walls. We have passed a terrible night — a night of horror, a night of suffering, a night to try the nerves of the strongest men.

143

"The fire broke out about twenty minutes before twelve o'clock Saturday night and was first seen breaking through the rear of the upper part of the opera house situated on the corner of Sixth and Territorial Streets, the alarm being immediately given.

"There had been a performance in the hall during the evening, the drama of *The Factory Girl* being given to a good- sized audience. The latter had not all departed from the opera house more than half an hour when the flames were first seen."

Karla's hand shook as she dialed Cynthia's telephone number. Cynthia picked it up on the second ring.

"Listen to this," Karla said and she read the first two paragraphs aloud. Cynthia remained silent as Karla continued reading:

"The origin of the fire is a mystery, and accounts differ as to whether it started on or under the stage, or in the lower story, and whether from a match or cigar stub carelessly thrown aside, a lamp or candle overturned, a live electric wire or other cause. Testimony so far taken before the coroner's jury would seem to indicate that it started in the *News* office.

"The coroner's inquest may reveal the commencement of a conflagration that in one short hour destroyed $52,900 worth of property and blotted out twelve human lives.

"Mr. J.A. Simon, office manager of the opera house, had started out after the show to post bills for another performance to be given Monday night, and was one of the first to see the blaze and give the alarm. He says there was no lamp or candle used about the stage, so that the fire could not have caught from that cause. He does not know how the fire originated."

Karla stopped reading at the end of the section. She could hear the reassuring sound of Cynthia's steady breathing. "Poor Mr. Simon," Karla said, reverting to the syntax of the Victorian age. "I wonder what he's doing now?"

"Karla," Cynthia said gently. "That was years ago, remember?"

"Right. Only sometimes it seems like yesterday. I can so easily summon the memories of peace and quiet in the orchards. Well, you know."

Karla was struck out of her reverie by a sobering thought.

144

"Cynthia, should we have told the truth about the origin of the fire?" she asked, hearing her voice quavering. Doily climbed into her lap. How did animals always know when comfort was needed, Karla wondered? She hugged the cat gratefully.

"I don't know, Karla. Some things are meant to be. We did our best to help the people involved and I think we made the right choice. What good would it have done to implicate Will McClanahan?"

"You're right. He wouldn't have had to live with the consequences, but his family and Emily Carter would have."

"Is there more to the story?"

"It's long."

"I'd like to hear the rest, if you don't mind reading it."

Karla continued reading: "The fire was burning for at least ten minutes before it burst out in a visible flame, but meantime a score of people had seen the smoke or blaze or heard the first alarm and were spreading the thrilling news that the opera house block was on fire. The alarm was first sounded from the city hall by persons unknown and was taken up by locomotives and other whistles and bells about the city. The people began to gather and before the flames broke out to any extent and while the smoking block was still intact a crowd of hundreds that afterwards swelled to two or three thousand were surging about the vicinity of the fire on all sides of the burning structure.

"The rattle of the hose carts, shouts of the firemen, cries of spectators, clatter of horses' hoofs on the pavements, rumble of vehicles and other sounds contributed to the general excitement.

"The fire department promptly responded to the alarm and many lines of hose were laid, every hydrant in the vicinity being pressed in service. Soon after midnight the flames broke through the roof and illumined the sky and streets with a lurid glare that only served to make more vivid the general scene of confusion and excitement.

"As soon as the flames broke through the windows and walls and let in the draft, the burning block was known to be doomed, and soon became a fiery furnace, and consternation took the place of anxiety as the possibility of destruction with the high wind gave rise to wild fears and speculations. Fortunately, however, the labors of the firemen proved of avail and the constant deluge of water on the opera house and adjacent blocks kept the fire confined to the four story Yore building and the two story Frick block adjoining, both of which were completely destroyed.

"Falling walls proved to be not only death traps for the fire fighters but dangerous for everyone who was trying to help stay the progress of the flames or assist in saving goods. The first to go down was the top part of the alley wall which buried in its cruel, crushing descent with tons of debris fifteen brave firemen."

Karla gasped and drew a long breath before continuing:

"This terrible sight was witnessed by at least a hundred horror stricken spectators, who stood helplessly looking at the distressing catastrophe and many of whom rushed in regardless of further danger of fire and smoke to help the shrieking and struggling men.

"The dead are Silas F. Watson, John Hoffman, Thomas Kidd, Jacob Franklin Woodley, Edward H. Gange, Scott Rice, Will Mittan, Louis Hoffman, Arthur C. Hill, Frank Seaver, Robert A. L. Rofe, Will McCormick.

"'Just before the wall fell,' says Mr. W. N. Chadsey, 'they were trying to raise the ladders and had got them against the building when the wall tumbled in, sweeping everything flat. You could see portions of human bodies through the fallen bricks. Parties going in to save the imprisoned men were overcome by the heat. The first man who went in simply spun around like a top in the intense heat and had to retreat. Finally one gray-headed man I do not know persisted in remaining in the ruins, working for the buried firemen. Then others hurried to the rescue. The wall had scarcely fallen when Dr. Bostick ran down the stairs in the rear of the Hulbard block to the assistance of the men. He summoned the help of Dr. Goodhart. There must have been nearly twenty men in the alley when the wall fell.'

"The other walls of the opera house fell subsequently, the front wall standing the longest, that falling at 2:30 a.m. At this writing — Monday — there is left standing of the opera house block only the walls of the lower story with the partition walls and portions of the alley and the west walls.

"Sparks fell in all directions, principally to the east, but these

146

were closely watched and before the east wall of the big block had fallen all the wooden buildings across Sixth Street had been saturated and the fire did not cross the street. The buildings on the north side of Territorial Road were not in danger at any time.

"The Yore block was occupied by the opera house (which took in all of the building except three storerooms in the lower story) and by Mr. J. Bernstein with a clothing stock in the corner store and the *Evening News* in the center store, the west store room being unoccupied. In the rear of Bernstein's store were S. M. Austin's bakery and John Holmes' barber shop, opening on Sixth Street.

"Mr. Bernstein was a new-comer and had a small stock. The proprietor and clerk were so excited that the firemen had to turn the hose on them to get them out of the burning block.

"The *Evening News* was owned principally by Mr. J. N. Klock, who bought it a year ago from its founder, Mr. J. W. McEachren. Everything about the office was completely destroyed — the presses, type, racks, stones, furniture, etc.

"Butzbach & Schutz and Jeff Dalrymple had apple barrels stored in the Yore block, the former in the basement and Mr. Dalrymple in the vacant store room. They lost about $800 worth of their goods, about evenly divided as to ownership and with no insurance.

"The Frick building which was the only one entirely consumed aside from the Yore block was a neat, comparatively new brick structure owned by Joseph Frick and occupied below by his shoe and repair shop and above in the upper story by his family as a residence. They saved very little of the shoe stock or household goods. Mr. Frick will open up another store in a few days in another location.

"Daniels Bros.' barber shop in the basement of the Frick building was a total loss. There was no insurance.

"The upper story of the Grocers' block was occupied besides the grocers above named, by the families of Messrs. Hunt and Austin over their respective stores and by Mrs. Jacob Smith and Mr. and Mrs. Asa Lester over Herr Brothers. The household goods and effects of all of these families were partially removed and were all more or less damaged by the water with which the block was flooded.

"The adjoining building west of Frick's was Schuder & Stein's saloon; a story and a half wooden building, which escaped. It was kept flooded. They took out part of the contents. John Schuder roomed overhead.

"Everything that could be carried was taken from Thayer & Company's one story fruit package office adjoining, but nothing was damaged here or in the other buildings further west.

"Some household goods were taken out of the Hanson and Hulburd blocks adjoining the Grocers' block on the west, but no material damage was done in or about those blocks.

"A number of guests of the Hotel Benton removed their belongings but returned to the hotel when the fire was brought under control.

"The fire was under control at three o'clock and by four o'clock it was reduced to a smouldering and ghastly ruin. Words cannot express the appalling force of this great horror, the sorrow in the stricken homes, or the shadow of grief that rested on this peaceful community on Sabbath morning."

Karla put the yellowed newspaper on the countertop and smoothed its creases. The paper's edges were ragged.

"You know," Cynthia said. "When we were there, I thought I knew everyone in town, but I didn't know half of the people mentioned in that story."

"We get wrapped up in our own little worlds and forget that there are so many others. I think I'll frame this newspaper and hang it in the shop, as a memorial to all of those people."

"To Miss Emily Carter, and to Miss Lily."

"Especially to them. And to Grace and Dan and Theodora."

"How about Sheriff Knapp?"

"Oh, sure. Why not? To him, too!"

THE END

About the Contributors ...

Author *Kathryn Schultz Zerler* lives on Lake Michigan with her husband Glenn Zerler and their black lab mix Maxine, their golden lab mix Sandy, and Polly the cat. She is Executive Director of St. Joseph Today and an adjunct faculty member at Lake Michigan College.

Historical Consultant *Nancy Watts-Stiles* lives in Niles, Michigan with her husband D. Wayne Stiles, her daughter Jennifer, and their cat Chemise. Along with her consulting services, she serves as Educational Coordinator at the Fort St. Joseph Museum in Niles.

Book Designer *Joann Phillips* lives in Niles, Michigan with her husband Rick Phillips. They have two daughters, Tracy and Jennifer. She is Marketing Director at Lake Michigan College, and a workout wonder woman.

Cover Designer *Vicky Nemethy* lives in St. Joseph, Michigan with her husband John Nemethy. They have two daughters, Kristeen and Sheila, and two grandchildren. She is the owner of Gallery on the Alley in downtown St. Joseph.

*For information on purchasing
this book, contact:*

*The Sleeping Cat Press
P.O. Box 251
St. Joseph, Michigan 49085
(616) 983-0077*

For information on purchasing:

On the Banks of the Ole St. Joe
and
Talk of The Towns

contact:

*St. Joseph Today
520 Pleasant Street
St. Joseph, Michigan 49085*

(616) 923-6739